Within a few hundred yards, it became apparent that she had an escort. She didn't look around for them, but they spread out to the right and left like a skirmish line, keeping abreast with her. Occasional shadows slid silently through patches of open, sunlit ground, disappeared again under the trees. . . .

Wisps of thought which were not her own thoughts flicked through Telzey's mind from moment to moment as the silent line of shadows moved deeper into the park with her. She realized she was being sized up, judged, evaluated again. . . . This was the first human mind that hadn't seemed deaf and silent to their form of communication. They were taking time out to study it . . . They were curious and they liked games. At the moment, Telzey, and what she might try to do to change their plans, was the game on which their attention was fixed. . . .

But what is a game to the telepathic Crest Cats is deadly earnest to the human race—and Telzey Amberdon must walk the perilous line between alien intelligence and human government if she doesn't want to find herself abandoned by them both.

Other Ace Science Fiction Books by James H. Schmitz

AGENT OF VEGA
THE WITCHES OF KARRES

The Telzey Amberdon Series

THE UNIVERSE AGAINST HER
THE TELZEY TOY AND OTHER STORIES (coming in December 1984)
THE LION GAME (coming in January 1985)

The Universe Against Her

James H. Schmitz

ACE SCIENCE FICTION BOOKS
NEW YORK

THE UNIVERSE AGAINST HER

An Ace Science Fiction Book / published by arrangement with
the Estate of James H. Schmitz

PRINTING HISTORY
Ace edition / April 1979
Fourth printing / November 1984

ISBN: 0-441-84577-0

Ace Science Fiction Books are published by The Berkley Publishing Group,
200 Madison Avenue, New York, New York 10016.
PRINTED IN THE UNITED STATES OF AMERICA

This book is for Betty

PART ONE

I

THERE WAS, Telzey Amberdon thought, someone besides TT and herself in the garden. Not, of course, Aunt Halet, who was in the house waiting for an early visitor to arrive, and not one of the servants. Someone or something else must be concealed among the thickets of magnificently flowering native Jontarou shrubs about Telzey.

She could think of no other way to account for Tick-Tock's spooked behavior—nor, to be honest about it, for the manner in which her own nerves were acting up without visible cause this morning.

Telzey plucked a blade of grass, slipped the end between her lips and chewed it gently, her face puzzled and concerned. She wasn't ordinarily afflicted with nervousness. Fifteen years old, genius level, brown as a berry and not at all bad looking in her sunbriefs, she was the youngest member of one of Orado's most prominent families and a second-year law student at one of the most exclusive schools in the Federation of the Hub. Her physical, mental, and emotional health, she'd always been informed, was excellent. Aunt Halet's frequent cracks about the in-

1

herent instability of the genius level could be ignored; Halet's own stability seemed questionable at best.

But none of that made the present odd situation any less disagreeable. . . .

The trouble might have begun, Telzey decided, during the night, within an hour after they arrived from the spaceport at the guest house Halet had rented in Port Nichay for their vacation on Jontarou. Telzey had retired at once to her second-story bedroom with Tick-Tock, but she barely got to sleep before something awakened her again. Turning over, she discovered TT reared up before the window, her forepaws on the sill, big cat-head outlined against the star-hazed night sky, staring fixedly down into the garden.

Telzey, only curious at that point, climbed out of bed and joined TT at the window. There was nothing in particular to be seen, and if the scents and minor night-sounds which came from the garden weren't exactly what they were used to, Jontarou was after all an unfamiliar planet. What else would one expect here?

But Tick-Tock's muscular back felt tense and rigid when Telzey laid her arms across it, and except for an absent-minded dig with her forehead against Telzey's shoulder, TT refused to let her attention be distracted from whatever had absorbed it. Now and then, a low, ominous rumble came from her furry throat, a half-angry, half-questioning sound. Telzey began to feel a little uncomfortable. She managed finally to coax Tick-Tock away from the window, but neither of them slept well the rest of the night. At breakfast,

Aunt Halet made one of her typical nasty-sweet remarks.

"You look so fatigued, dear, as if you were under some severe mental strain . . . which, of course, you might be." With her gold-blond hair piled high on her head and her peaches-and-cream complexion, Halet looked fresh as a daisy herself . . . a malicious daisy. "Now wasn't I right in insisting to Jessamine that you needed a vacation away from that terribly intellectual school?" She smiled gently.

"Absolutely," Telzey agreed, restraining the impulse to fling a spoonful of egg yolk at her father's younger sister. Aunt Halet often inspired such impulses, but Telzey had promised her mother to avoid actual battles on the Jontarou trip, if possible. After breakfast, she went out into the back garden with Tick-Tock, who immediately walked into a thicket, camouflaged herself and vanished from sight. It seemed to add up to something. But what?

Telzey strolled about the garden a while, maintaining a pretense of nonchalant interest in Jontarou's flowers and colorful bug life. She experienced the most curious little chills of alarm from time to time, but discovered no signs of a lurking intruder, or of TT either. Then, for half an hour or more, she'd just sat cross-legged in the grass, waiting quietly for Tick-Tock to show up of her own accord. And the big lunkhead hadn't obliged.

Telzey scratched a tanned kneecap, scowling at Port Nichay's park trees beyond the garden wall. It seemed idiotic to feel scared when she couldn't even tell whether there was anything to be scared about! And, aside from that, another unreasonable feeling kept growing stronger by the minute now. This was to the effect that she should be doing some unstated but specific thing. . . .

In fact, that Tick-Tock *wanted* her to do some specific thing!

Completely idiotic!

Abruptly, Telzey closed her eyes and thought sharply, "Tick-Tock?" and waited—suddenly very angry at herself for having given in to her fancies to this extent—for whatever might happen.

She had never really established that she was able to tell, by a kind of symbolic mind-picture method, like a short waking dream, approximately what TT was thinking and feeling. Five years before, when she'd discovered Tick-Tock—an odd-looking and odder-behaved stray kitten then—in the woods near the Amberdons' summer home on Orado, Telzey had thought so. But it might never have been more than a colorful play of her imagination; and after she got into law school and grew increasingly absorbed in her studies, she almost forgot the matter again.

Today, perhaps because she was disturbed about Tick-Tock's behavior, the customary response was extraordinarily prompt. The warm glow of sunlight shining through her closed eyelids faded out quickly and was replaced by some inner darkness. In the darkness there appeared then an image of Tick-Tock sitting a little way off beside an open door in an old stone wall, green eyes fixed on Telzey. Telzey got the impression that TT was inviting her to go through the door, and, for some reason, the thought frightened her.

Again, there was an immediate reaction. The scene with Tick-Tock and the door vanished; and Telzey felt she was standing in a pitch-black room, knowing that if she moved even one step forward, something that was waiting there silently would reach out and grab her.

Naturally, she recoiled . . . and at once found herself sitting, eyes still closed and the sunlight bathing her lids, in the grass of the guest house garden.

She opened her eyes, looked around. Her heart was thumping rapidly. The experience couldn't have lasted more than four or five seconds, but it had been extremely vivid, a whole, compact little nightmare. None of her earlier experiments at getting into mental communication with TT had been like that.

It served her right, Telzey thought, for trying such a childish stunt at the moment! What she should have done at once was to make a methodical search for the foolish beast—TT was bound to be *somewhere* nearby—locate her behind her camouflage, and hang on to her then until this nonsense in the garden was explained! Talented as Tick-Tock was at blotting herself out, it usually was possible to spot her if one directed one's attention to shadow patterns. Telzey began a surreptitious study of the clusters of flowering bushes about her.

Three minutes later, off to her right, where the ground was banked beneath a six-foot step in the garden's terraces. Tick-Tock's outline suddenly caught her eye. Flat on her belly, head lifted above her paws, quite motionless, TT seemed like a transparent wraith stretched out along the terrace, barely discernible even when stared at directly. It was a convincing illusion; but what seemed to be rocks, plant leaves, and sun-splotched earth seen through the wraith-outline was simply the camouflage pattern TT had printed for the moment on her hide. She could have changed it completely in an instant to conform to a different background.

Telzey pointed an accusing finger.

"See you!" she announced, feeling a surge of relief which seemed as unaccountable as the rest of it.

The wraith twitched one ear in acknowledgement, the head outlines shifting as the camouflaged face turned towards Telzey. Then the inwardly uncamouflaged, very substantial looking mouth opened slowly, showing Tick-Tock's red tongue and curved white tusks. The mouth stretched in a wide yawn, snapped shut with a click of meshing teeth, became indistinguishable again. Next, a pair of camouflaged lids drew back from TT's round, brilliant-green eyes. The eyes stared across the lawn at Telzey.

Telzey said irritably, "Quit clowning around, TT!"

The eyes blinked, and Tick-Tock's natural bronze-brown color suddenly flowed over her head, down her neck and across her body into legs and tail. Against the side of the terrace, as if materializing into solidity at that moment, appeared two hundred pounds of supple, rangy, long-tailed cat . . . or catlike creature.

TT's actual origin had never been established. The best guesses were that what Telzey had found playing around in the woods five years ago was either a biostructural experiment which had got away from a private laboratory on Orado, or some spaceman's lost pet, brought to the capital planet from one of the remote colonies beyond the Hub. On top of TT's head was a large, fluffy pompon of white fur, which might have looked ridiculous on another animal, but didn't on her. Even as a fat kitten, hanging head down from the side of a wall by the broad sucker pads in her paws, TT had possessed enormous dignity.

Telzey studied her, the feeling of relief fading again. Tick-Tock, ordinarily the most restful and composed of companions, definitely was still tensed up about something. That big, lazy yawn a moment ago, the attitude of stretched-out relaxation . . . all pure sham!

"What is eating you?" she asked in exasperation.

The green eyes stared at her, solemn, watchful, seeming for that fleeting instant quite alien. And why, Telzey thought, should the old question of what Tick-Tock really was pass through her mind just now? After her rather alarming rate of growth began to taper off last year, nobody had cared any more. She was simply Tick-Tock. . . .

For a moment, Telzey had the uncanny certainty of having had the answer to this situation almost in her grasp. An answer which appeared to involve the world of Jontarou, Tick-Tock, and of all unlikely factors . . . Aunt Halet.

She shook her head. TT's impassive green eyes blinked.

Jontarou? The planet lay outside Telzey's sphere of personal interests, but she'd read up on it on the way here from Orado. Among all the worlds of the Hub, Jontarou was the paradise for zoologists and sportsmen, a gigantic animal preserve, its continents and seas swarming with magnificent game. Under Federation law, it was retained deliberately in the primitive state in which it had been discovered. Port Nichay, the only city, actually the only inhabited point on Jontarou, was beautiful and quiet, a pattern of vast but elegantly slender towers, each separated from the others by four or five miles of rolling parkland and interconnected only by the threads of transparent skyways. Near the horizon, just visible from the garden, rose the tallest towers of all, the green and gold spires of the Shikaris' Club, a center of Federation affairs and of social activity. From the aircar which brought them across Port Nichay the evening before, Telzey had seen occasional strings of guest houses, similar to the one Halet had rented, nestling along the park slopes.

Nothing very sinister about Port Nichay or green Jontarou, surely!

Halet? That blond, slinky, would-be Machiavelli? What could. . . ?

Telzey's eyes narrowed reflectively. There'd been a minor occurrence—at least, it had seemed minor—just before the spaceliner docked last night. A young woman from one of the newscasting services had asked for an interview with the daughter of Federation Councilwoman Jessamine Amberdon. This happened occasionally; and Telzey had no objections until the newsmen's gossipy persistence in inquiring about the "unusual pet" she was bringing to Port Nichay with her began to be annoying. TT might be somewhat unusual, but that was not a matter of general interest, and Telzey said so. Then Halet moved smoothly into the act and held forth on Tick-Tock's appearance, habits, and mysterious antecedents, in considerable detail.

Telzey had assumed that Halet was simply going out of her way to be irritating, as usual. Looking back on the incident, however, it occurred to her that the chatter between her aunt and the newscast woman had sounded oddly stilted—almost like something the two might have rehearsed.

Rehearsed for what purpose? Tick-Tock . . . Jontarou . . .

Telzey chewed gently on her lower lip. A vacation on Jontarou for the two of them and TT had been Halet's idea, and Halet had enthused about it so much that Telzey's mother at last talked her into accepting. Halet, Jessamine explained privately to Telzey, had felt they were intruders in the Amberdon family, had bitterly resented Jessamine's political honors and, more recently, Telzey's own emerging promise of brilliance. This invitation was Halet's way of indicating a change of heart. Wouldn't Telzey oblige?

So Telzey had obliged, though she took very little stock in Halet's change of heart. She wasn't, in fact, putting it past her aunt to have some involved dirty trick up her sleeve with this trip to Jontarou. Halet's mind worked like that.

So far there had been no actual indications of purposeful mischief. But logic did seem to require a connection between the various puzzling events here, especially the newscaster's rather forced looking interest in Tick-Tock. Halet could easily have paid for that interview. Then TT's disturbed behavior during their first night in Port Nichay, and Telzey's own formless anxieties and fancies in connection with the guest house garden.

The last remained hard to explain. But Tick-Tock ... and Halet ... might know something about Jontarou that she didn't know.

Her mind returned to the results of the half-serious attempt she'd made to find out whether there was something Tick-Tock "wanted her to do." An open door? A darkness where somebody wanted to grab her if she took even one step forward? It couldn't have had any significance. Or could it?

So you'd like to try magic, Telzey scoffed at herself. Baby games ... How far would you have got at law school if you'd asked TT to help with your problems?

Then why had she been thinking about it again?

She shivered, because an eerie stillness seemed to settle on the garden. From the side of the terrace, TT's green eyes watched her.

Telzey had a feeling of sinking down slowly into a sunlit dream, into something very remote from law school problems.

"Should I go through the door?" she whispered.

The bronze cat-shape raised its head slowly. TT began to purr.

Tick-Tock's name had been derived in kittenhood from the manner in which she purred—a measured, oscillating sound, shifting from high to low, as comfortable and often as continuous as the unobtrusive pulse of an old clock. It was the first time, Telzey realized now, that she'd heard the sound since their arrival on Jontarou. It went on for a dozen seconds or so, then stopped. Tick-Tock continued to look at her.

It appeared to have been an expression of definite assent. . . .

The dreamlike sensation increased, hazing over Telzey's thoughts. If there was nothing to this mind-communication thing, what harm could symbols do? This time, she wouldn't let them alarm her. And if they did mean something . . .

She closed her eyes.

II

THE SUNGLOW outside faded instantly. Telzey caught a fleeting picture of the door in the wall, and knew in the same moment that she'd already passed through it.

She was not in the dark room then, but poised at the edge of a brightness which seemed featureless and without limit, spread out around her with a feeling-tone like "sea" or "sky." But it was an unquiet place. There was a sense of unseen things on all sides watching her and waiting.

Was this another form of the dark room—a trap set up in her mind? Telzey's attention did a quick shift. She was seated in the grass again; the sunlight beyond her closed eyelids seemed to shine in quietly through rose-tinted curtains. Cautiously, she let her awareness return to the bright area; and *it* was still there. She had a moment of excited elation. She was controlling this! And why not, she asked herself. These things were happening in *her* mind, after all!

She would find out what they seemed to mean; but she would be in no rush to . . .

An impression as if, behind her, Tick-Tock had thought, "Now I can help again!"

Then a feeling of being swept swiftly, irresistibly forward, thrust out and down. The brightness exploded in thundering colors around her. In fright, she made the effort to snap her eyes open, to be back in the garden; but now she couldn't make it work. The colors continued to roar about her, like a confusion of excited, laughing, triumphant voices. Telzey felt caught in the middle of it all, suspended in invisible spider webs. Tick-Tock seemed to be somewhere nearby, looking on. Faithless, treacherous TT!

Telzey's mind made another wrenching effort, and there was a change. She hadn't got back into the garden, but the noisy, swirling colors were gone and she had the feeling of reading a rapidly moving microtape now, though she didn't actually see the tape.

The tape, she realized, was another symbol for what was happening, a symbol easier for her to understand. There were voices, or what might be voices, around her; on the invisible tape she seemed to be reading what they said.

A number of speakers, apparently involved in a fast, hot argument about what to do with her. Impressions flashed past. . . .

Why waste time with her? It was clear that kitten-talk was all she was capable of! . . . Not necessarily; that was a normal first step. Give her a little time! . . . But what—exasperatedly—could such a small-bite possibly know that would be of significant value?

There was a slow, blurred, awkward-seeming interruption. Its content was not comprehensible to Telzey at all, but in some unmistakable manner it was defined as Tick-Tock's thought.

A pause as the circle of speakers stopped to consider whatever TT had thrown into the debate.

Then another impression . . . one that sent a

shock of fear through Telzey as it rose heavily into her awareness. Its sheer intensity momentarily displaced the tape-reading symbolism. A savage voice seemed to rumble:

"Toss the tender small-bite to *me*"—malevolent crimson eyes fixed on Telzey from somewhere not far away—"and let's be done here!"

Startled, stammering protest from Tick-Tock, accompanied by gusts of laughter from the circle. Great sense of humor these characters had. Telzey thought bitterly. That crimson-eyed thing wasn't joking at all!

More laughter as the circle caught her thought. Then a kind of majority opinion found sudden expression:

"Small-bite *is* learning! No harm to wait. . . . We'll find out quickly. . . ."

The tape ended; the voices faded; the colors went blank. In whatever jumbled-up form she'd been getting the impressions at that point— Telzey couldn't have begun to describe it—the whole thing suddenly stopped.

She found herself sitting in the grass, shaky, scared, eyes open. Tick-Tock stood beside the terrace, looking at her. An air of hazy unreality still hung about the garden.

She might have flipped! She didn't think so; but it certainly seemed possible! Otherwise . . . Telzey made an attempt to sort over what had happened.

Something *had* been in the garden! Something had been inside her mind. Something that was at home on Jontarou.

There'd been a feeling of perhaps fifty or sixty of these . . . well, beings. Alarming beings! Reckless, wild, hard . . . and that red-eyed nightmare! Telzey shuddered.

They'd contacted Tick-Tock first, during the night. TT understood them better than she could. Why? Telzey found no immediate answer.

Then Tick-Tock had tricked her into letting her mind be invaded by these beings. There must have been a very definite reason for that.

She looked over at Tick-Tock. TT looked back. Nothing stirred in Telzey's thoughts. Between *them* there was still no direct communication.

Then how had the beings been able to get through to her?

Telzey wrinkled her nose. Assuming this was real, it seemed clear that the game of symbols she'd made up between herself and TT had provided the openings. Her whole experience just now had been in the form of symbols, translating whatever occurred into something she could consciously grasp.

"Kitten-talk" was how the beings referred to the use of symbols; they seemed contemptuous of it. Never mind, Telzey told herself; they'd agreed she was learning.

The air over the grass appeared to flicker. Again she had the impression of reading words off a quickly moving, not quite visible tape.

"You're being taught and you're learning," was what she seemed to read. "The question was whether you were capable of partial understanding as your friend insisted. Since you were, everything else that can be done will be accomplished quickly." A pause, then with a touch of approval, "You've a well-formed mind, small-bite! Odd and with incomprehensibilities, but well-formed . . ."

One of the beings, and a fairly friendly one—at least not unfriendly. Telzey framed a tentative mental question. "Who are you?"

"You'll know very soon." The flickering ended; she realized she and the question had been dismissed for the moment. She looked over at Tick-Tock again.

"Can't you talk to me now, TT?" she asked silently.

A feeling of hesitation.

"Kitten-talk!" was the impression that formed itself with difficulty then. It was awkward, searching, but it came unquestionably from TT. "Still learning, too, Telzey!" TT seemed half anxious, half angry. "We . . ."

A sharp buzz-note reached Telzey's ears, wiping out the groping thought-impression. She jumped a little, glanced down. Her wrist-talker was signaling. For a moment, she seemed poised uncertainly between a world where unseen, dangerous-sounding beings referred to one as "small-bite" and where TT was learning to talk, and the familiar other world where wrist-communicators buzzed periodically in a matter-of-fact manner. Settling back into the more familiar world, she switched on the talker.

"Yes?" she said. Her voice sounded husky.

"Telzey, dear," Halet murmured honey-sweet from the talker. "would you come back into the house, please? The living room. We have a visitor who very much wants to meet you."

Telzey hesitated, eyes narrowing. Halet's visitor wanted to meet her?"

"Why?" she asked.

"He has something very interesting to tell you, dear." The edge of triumphant malice showed for an instant, vanished in murmuring sweetness again. "So please hurry!"

"All right." Telzey stood up. "I'm coming."

"Fine, dear!" The talker went dead.

Telzey switched off the instrument, noticed that Tick-Tock had chosen to disappear meanwhile.

Flipped? She wondered, starting up towards the house. It was clear Aunt Halet had prepared some unpleasant surprise to spring on her, which was hardly more than normal behavior for Halet. The other business? She couldn't be certain of anything there. Leaving out TT's strange actions—which might have a number of causes, after all—that entire string of events could have been created inside her head. There was no contradictory evidence so far.

But it could do no harm to take what seemed to have happened at face value. Some pretty grim event might be shaping up, in a very real way, around here. . . .

"You reason logically!" The impression now was of a voice speaking to her, a voice that made no audible sound. It was the same being who'd addressed her a minute or two ago.

The two worlds between which Telzey had felt suspended seemed to glide slowly together and become one.

"I go to law school," she explained to the being, almost absently.

Amused agreement. "So we heard."

"What do you want of me?" Telzey inquired.

"You'll know soon enough."

"Why not tell me now?" Telzey urged. It seemed about to dismiss her again.

Quick impatience flared at her. "Kitten-pictures! Kitten-thoughts! Kitten-talk! Too slow, too slow! YOUR pictures—too much YOU! Wait till the . . ."

Circuits close . . . channels open . . . Obstructions clear? What *had* it said? There'd been only the blurred image of a finicky, delicate, but perfectly normal technical operation of some kind.

". . . minutes now!" the voice concluded. A pause, then another thought tossed carelessly at her. "This is more important to you, small-bite, than to us!" The voice impression ended as sharply as if a communicator had snapped off.

Not *too* friendly! Telzey walked on towards the house, a new fear growing inside her . . . a fear like the awareness of a storm gathered nearby, still quiet—deadly quiet, but ready to break.

"Kitten-pictures!" a voice seemed to jeer distantly, a whispering in the park trees beyond the garden wall.

Halet's cheeks were lightly pinked; her blue eyes sparkled. She looked downright stunning, which meant to anyone who knew her that the worst side of Halet's nature was champing at the bit again. On uninformed males it had a dazzling effect, however; and Telzey wasn't surprised to find their visitor wearing a tranced expression when she came into the living room. He was a tall, outdoorsy man with a tanned, bony face, a neatly trained black mustache, and a scar down one cheek which would have seemed dashing if it hadn't been for the stupefied look. Beside his chair stood a large, clumsy instrument which might have been some kind of tele-camera.

Halet performed introductions. Their visitor was Dr. Droon, a zoologist. He had been tuned in on Telzey's newscast interview on the liner the night before, and wondered whether Telzey would care to discuss Tick-Tock with him.

"Frankly, no," Telzey said.

Dr. Droon came awake and gave Telzey a surprised look. Halet smiled easily.

"My niece doesn't intend to be discourteous, doctor," she explained.

"Of course not," the zoologist agreed doubtfully.

"It's just," Halet went on, "that Telzey is a little, oh, sensitive where Tick-Tock is concerned. In her own way, she's attached to the animal. Aren't you, dear?"

"Yes," Telzey said blandly.

"Well, we hope this isn't going to disturb you too much, dear." Halet glanced significantly at Dr. Droon. "Dr. Droon, you must understand, is simply doing . . . well, there is something very important he must tell you now."

Telzey transferred her gaze back to the zoologist. Dr. Droon cleared his throat. "I, ah, understand, Miss Amberdon, that you're unaware of what kind of creature your, ah, Tick-Tock is?"

Telzey started to speak, then checked herself, frowning. She had been about to state that she knew exactly what kind of creature TT was . . . but she didn't, of course!

Or did she? She . . .

She scowled absentmindedly at Dr. Droon, biting her lip.

"Telzey!" Halet prompted gently.

"Huh?" Telzey said. "Oh ... please go on, doctor!"

Dr. Droon steepled his fingers. "Well," he said, "she—your pet—is, ah, a young crest cat. Nearly full grown now, apparently, and ..."

"Why, yes!" Telzey cried.

The zoologist looked at her. "You knew that ..."

"Well, not really," Telzey admitted. "Or sort of." She laughed, her cheeks flushed. "This is the most ... go ahead, please! Sorry I interrupted." She stared at the wall beyond Dr. Droon with a rapt expression.

The zoologist and Halet exchanged glances. Then Dr. Droon resumed cautiously. The crest cats, he said, were a species native to Jontarou. Their existence had been known for only eight years. The species appeared to have had a somewhat limited range—the Baluit mountains on the opposite side of the huge continent on which Port Nichay had been built. . . .

Telzey barely heard him. A very curious thing was happening. For every sentence Dr. Droon uttered, a dozen other sentences appeared in her awareness. More accurately, it was as if an instantaneous smooth flow of information relevant to whatever he said arose continuously from what might have been almost her own memory, but wasn't. Within a minute or two, she knew more about the crest cats of Jontarou than Dr. Droon could have told her in hours ... much more than he'd ever known.

She realized suddenly that he'd stopped talking, that he had asked her a question. "Miss Amberdon?" he repeated now, with a note of uncertainty.

"Yar-rrr-REE!" Telzey told him softly. "I'll drink your blood!"

"Eh?"

Telzey blinked, focused on Dr. Droon, wrenching her mind away from a splendid view of the misty-blue peaks of the Baluit range. . . .

"Sorry," she said briskly. "Just a joke!" She smiled. "Now what were you saying?"

The zoologist looked at her in a rather odd manner for a moment. "I was inquiring," he said then, "whether you were familiar with the sporting rules established by the various hunting associations of the Hub in connection with the taking of game trophies?"

Telzey shook her head, "No, I never heard of them."

The rules, Dr. Droon explained, laid down the type of equipment—weapons, spotting and tracking instruments, number of assistants, and so forth—a sportsman could legitimately use in the pursuit of any specific type of game. "Before the end of the first year after their discovery," he went on, "the Baluit crest cats had been placed in the ultra-equipment class."

"What's ultra-equipment?" Telzey asked.

"Well," Dr. Droon said thoughtfully, "it doesn't quite involve the use of full battle armor . . . not quite! And, of course, even with that classification, the sporting principle of mutual accessibility must be observed."

"Mutual . . . oh, I see!" Telzey paused as

another wave of silent information rose into her awareness; went on, "So the game has to be able to get at the sportsman too, eh?"

"That's correct. Except in the pursuit of various classes of flying animals, a shikari would not, for example, be permitted the use of an aircar other than as a means of simple transportation. Under these conditions, it was soon established that crest cats were being obtained by sportsmen who went after them at a rather consistent one-to-one ratio."

Telzey's eyes widened. She'd gathered something similar from her other information source but hadn't quite believed it. "One hunter killed for each cat bagged?" she said. "That's pretty rough sport, isn't it?"

"Extremely rough sport!" Dr. Droon agreed dryly. "In fact, when the statistics were published, the sporting interest in winning a Baluit cat trophy appears to have suffered a sudden and sharp decline. On the other hand, a more scientific interest in these remarkable animals was coincidingly created, and many permits for their acquisition by the agents of museums, universities, public and private collections were issued. Sporting rules, of course, do not apply to that activity. . . ."

Telzey nodded absently. "I see. They used aircars, didn't they? A sort of heavy knockout gun—"

"Aircars, long-range detectors and stunguns are standard equipment in such work," Dr. Droon acknowledged. "Gas and poison are employed, of course, as circumstances dictate. The collectors were relatively successful for a while. And then a curious thing happened. Less than two years after their existence became known, the crest cats of the Baluit range were extinct! The inroads made on their numbers by man cannot begin to account for this, so it must be assumed that a sudden plague wiped them out. At any rate, not another living member of the species has been seen on Jontarou until you landed here with your pet last night."

Telzey sat silent for some seconds. Not because of what he had said, but because the other knowledge was still flowing into her mind. On one very important point *that* was at variance with what the zoologist had stated, and from there a coldly logical pattern was building up. Telzey didn't grasp the pattern in complete detail yet, but what she saw of it stirred her with a half-incredulous dread.

She asked, shaping the words carefully, but with only a small part of her attention on what she was really saying, "Just what does all that have to do with Tick-Tock, Dr. Droon?"

Dr. Droon glanced at Halet, and returned his gaze to Telzey. Looking very uncomfortable but quite determined, he told her, "Miss Amberdon, there is a Federation law which states that when a species is threatened with extinction, any available survivors must be transferred to the Life Banks of the University League, to insure their indefinite preservation. Under the circumstances, this law applies to, ah, Tick-Tock!"

III

So that had been Halet's trick. . . . She'd found
out about the crest cats, might have put in as
much as a few months arranging to make the
discovery of TT's origin on Jontarou seem a re-
grettable mischance—something no one could
have foreseen or prevented. In the Life Banks,
from what Telzey had heard of them, TT would
cease to exist as an individual awareness while
scientists tinkered around with the possibilities
of reconstructing her species.

Telzey studied her aunt's carefully sympathiz-
ing face for an instant, then asked Dr. Droon,
"What about the other crest cats you said were
collected before they became extinct here?
Wouldn't they be enough for what the Life Banks
need?"

He shook his head. "Two immature male
specimens are known to exist, and they are at
present in the Life Banks. The others that were
taken alive at the time have been destroyed . . .
often under nearly disastrous circumstances.
They are enormously cunning, enormously savage creatures, Miss Amberdon! The additional
fact that they can conceal themselves to the point
of being virtually undetectable except by the use
of instruments makes them one of the most
dangerous animals known. Since the young
female which you raised as a pet has remained

24

docile, so far, you may not really be able to appreciate that."

"Perhaps I can," Telzey said. She nodded at the heavy-looking instrument standing beside his chair. "And that's . . ."

"It's a life detector combined with a stungun, Miss Amberdon. I have no intention of harming your pet, but we can't take chances with an animal of that type. The gun's charge will knock it unconscious for several minutes—just long enough to let me secure it with paralysis belts."

"You're a collector for the Life Banks, Dr. Droon?"

"That's correct."

"Dr. Droon," Halet remarked, "has obtained a permit from the Planetary Moderator, authorizing him to claim Tick-Tock for the University League and remove her from the planet, dear. So you see there is simply nothing we can do about the matter! Your mother wouldn't like us to attempt to obstruct the law, would she?" Halet paused. "The permit should have your signature, Telzey, but I can sign in your stead if necessary."

That was Halet's way of saying it would do no good to appeal to Jontarou's Planetary Moderator. She'd taken the precaution of getting his assent to the matter first.

"So now if you'll just call Tick-Tock, dear . . ." Halet went on.

Telzey barely heard the last words. She felt herself stiffening slowly, while the living room almost faded from her sight. Perhaps, in that instant, some additional new circuit had closed in her mind, or some additional new channel had opened, for TT's purpose in tricking her into contact with the reckless, mocking beings outside was suddenly and numbingly clear.

And what it meant immediately was that she'd have to get out of the house without being spotted at it, and go some place where she could be undisturbed for half an hour or more. . . .

She realized that Halet and the zoologist were both staring at her.

"Are you ill, dear?"

"No." Telzey stood up. It would be worse than useless to try to tell these two anything! Her face must be pretty white at the monent—she could feel it—but they assumed, of course, that the shock of losing TT had just now sunk in on her.

"I'll have to check on that law you mentioned before I sign anything," she told Dr. Droon.

"Why, yes . . ." He started to get out of his chair. "I'm sure that can be arranged, Miss Amberdon!"

"Don't bother to call the Moderator's office," Telzey said. "I brought my law library along. I'll look it up myself." She turned to leave the room.

"My niece," Halet explained to Dr. Droon who was beginning to look puzzled, "attends law school. She's always so absorbed in her studies . . . Telzey?"

"Yes, Halet?" Telzey paused at the door.

"I'm very glad you've decided to be sensible about this, dear. But don't take too long, will you? We don't want to waste Dr. Droon's time."

"It shouldn't take more than five or ten minutes," Telzey told her agreeably. She closed the door behind her, and went directly to her bedroom on the second floor. One of her two valises was still unpacked. She locked the door behind her, opened the unpacked valise, took out a pocket edition law library and sat down at the table with it.

She clicked on the library's viewscreen, tapped the clearing and index buttons. Behind the screen, one of the multiple rows of pinhead tapes shifted slightly as the index was flicked into reading position. Half a minute later, she was glancing over the legal section on which Dr. Droon had based his claim. The library confirmed what he had said.

Very neat of Halet, Telzey thought, very nasty . . . and pretty idiotic! Even a second-year law student could think immediately of two or three ways in which a case like that could have been dragged out in the Federation's courts for a couple of decades before the question of handing Tick-Tock over to the Life Banks became too acute.

Well, Halet simply wasn't really intelligent. And the plot to shanghai TT was hardly even a side issue now. . . .

Telzey snapped the tiny library shut, fastened it to the belt of her sunsuit and went over to the open window. A two-foot ledge passed beneath the window, leading to the roof of a patio on the right. Fifty yards beyond the patio, the garden ended in a natural stone wall. Behind it lay one of the big wooded park areas which formed most of the ground level of Port Nichay.

Tick-Tock wasn't in sight. A sound of voices came from ground-floor windows on the left. Halet had brought her maid and chauffeur along; and a chef had showed up in time to make breakfast this morning, as part of the city's guest house service. Telzey took the empty valise to the window, set it on end against the left side of the frame, and let the window slide down until its lower edge rested on the valise. She went back to the house guard-screen panel beside the door, put her finger against the lock button, and pushed.

The sound of voices from the lower floor was cut off as outer doors and windows slid silently shut all about the house. Telzey glanced back at the window. The valise had creaked a little as the guard field drove the frame down on it, but it was supporting the thrust. She returned to the window, wriggled feet foremost through the opening, twisted around and got a footing on the ledge.

A minute later, she was scrambling quietly down a vine-covered patio trellis to the ground. Even after they discovered she was gone, the guard screen would keep everybody in the house for some little while. They'd either have to disengage the screen's main mechanisms and start poking around in them, or force open the door to her bedroom and get the lock unset. Either approach would involve confusion, upset tempers, and generally delay any organized pursuit.

Telzey edged around the patio and started towards the wall, keeping close to the side of the house so she couldn't be seen from the windows. The shrubbery made minor rustling noises as she threaded her way through it . . . and then there was a different stirring which might have been no more than a slow, steady current of air moving among the bushes behind her. She shivered involuntarily but didn't look back.

She came to the wall, stood still, measuring its height, jumped and got an arm across it, swung up a knee and squirmed up and over. She came down on her feet with a small thump in the grass on the other side, glanced back once at the guest house, crossed a path and went on among the park trees.

Within a few hundred yards, it became apparent that she had an escort. She didn't look around for them, but they spread out to the right and left like a skirmish line, keeping abreast with her. Occasional shadows slid silently through patches of open, sunlit ground, disappeared again under the trees. Otherwise, there was hardly anyone in sight. Port Nichay's human residents appeared to make almost no personal use of the vast parkland spread out beneath their tower apartments; and its traffic moved over the airways, visible from the ground only as rainbow-hued ribbons which bisected the sky between the upper tower levels. An occasional private aircar went by overhead.

Wisps of thought which were not her own thoughts flicked through Telzey's mind from moment to moment as the silent line of shadows moved deeper into the park with her. She realized she was being sized up, judged, evaluated again. No more information was coming through; they had given her as much information as she needed. In the main perhaps, they were simply curious now. This was the first human mind they'd been able to make heads or tails of which hadn't seemed deaf and silent to their form of communication. They were taking time out to study it. They'd been assured she would have something of genuine importance to tell them; and there was some derision about that. But they were willing to wait a little, and find out. They were curious and they liked games. At the moment, Telzey, and what she might try to do to change their plans, was the game on which their attention was fixed.

Twelve minutes passed before the talker on Telzey's wrist began to buzz. It continued to signal off and on for another few minutes, then stopped. Back in the guest house they couldn't be sure yet whether she wasn't simply locked inside her room and refusing to answer them. But Telzey quickened her pace.

The park's trees gradually became more massive, reached higher above her, stood paced more widely apart. She passed through the morning shadow of the residential tower nearest the guest house, and emerged from it presently on the shore of a small lake. On the other side of the lake, a number of dappled grazing animals like long-necked, tall horses lifted their heads to watch her. For some seconds they seemed only mildly interested, but then a breeze moved across the lake, crinkling the surface of the water; and as it touched the opposite shore, abrupt panic exploded among the grazers. They wheeled, went flashing away in effortless twenty-foot strides, and were gone among the trees.

Telzey felt a crawling along her spine. It was the first objective indication she'd had of the nature of the company she had brought to the lake, and while it hardly came as a surprise, for a moment her urge was to follow the example of the grazers.

"Tick-Tock?" she whispered, suddenly a little short of breath.

A single up-and-down purring note replied from the bushes on her right. TT was still around, for whatever good that might do. Not too much, Telzey thought, if it came to serious trouble. But the knowledge was somewhat reassuring . . . and this, meanwhile, appeared to be as far as she needed to get from the guest house. They'd be looking for her by aircar presently, but there was nothing to tell them in which direction to turn first.

She climbed the bank of the lake to a point where she was screened both by thick, green shrubbery and the top of a single immense tree from the sky, sat down on some dry, mossy growth, took the law library from her belt, opened it and placed it in her lap. Vague stirrings indicated that her escort was also settling down in an irregular circle about her; and apprehension shivered on Telzey's skin again. It wasn't that their attitude was hostile; they were simply overawing. And no one could predict what they might do next. Without looking up, she asked a question in her mind.

"Ready?"

Sense of multiple acknowledgement, variously tinged—sardonic, interestedly amused, attentive, doubtful. Impatience quivered through it too, only tentatively held in restraint, and Telzey's forehead was suddenly wet. Some of them seemed on the verge of expressing disapproval with what was being done here.

Her fingers quickly flicked in the index tape, and the stir of feeling about her subsided, their attention captured again for the moment. Her thoughts became to some degree detached, ready to dissect another problem in the familiar ways and present the answers to it. Not a very involved problem essentially, but this time it wasn't a school exercise. Her company waited, withdrawn, silent, aloof once more, while the index blurred, checked, blurred and checked. Within a minute and a half, she had noted a dozen reference symbols. She tapped in another of the pinhead tapes, glanced over a few paragraphs, licked salty sweat from her lip, and said in her thoughts, emphasizing the meaning of each detail of the sentence so that there would be no misunderstanding, "This is the Federation law that applies to the situation which existed originally on this planet . . ."

There were no interruptions, no commenting thoughts, no intrusions of any kind, as she went step by step through the section, turned to another one, and another. In perhaps twelve minutes she came to the end of the last one, and stopped. Instantly, argument exploded about her.

Telzey was not involved in the argument; in fact, she could grasp only scraps of it. Either they were excluding her deliberately, or the exchange was too swift, practiced and varied to allow her to keep up. But their vehemence was not encouraging. And was it reasonable to assume that the Federation's laws would have any meaning for minds like these? Telzey snapped the library shut with fingers that had begun to tremble, and placed it on the ground. Then she stiffened. In the sensations washing about her, a special excitement rose suddenly, a surge of almost gleeful wildness that choked away her breath. Awareness followed of a pair of malignant crimson eyes fastened on her, moving steadily closer. A kind of nightmare paralysis seized Telzey—they'd turned her over to that red-eyed horror! She sat still, feeling mouse-sized.

Something came out with a crash from a thicket behind her. Her muscles went tight. But it was TT who rubbed a hard head against her shoulder, took another three stiff-legged steps forward and stopped between Telzey and the bushes on their right, back rigid, neck fur erect, tail twisting.

Expectant silence closed in about them. The circle was waiting. In the greenery on the right something made a slow, heavy stir.

TT's lips peeled back from her teeth. Her head swung towards the motion, ears flattening, transformed to a split, snarling demon-mask. A long shriek ripped from her lungs, raw with fury, blood lust and challenge.

The sound died away. For some seconds the tension about them held; then came a sense of gradual relaxation mingled with a partly amused approval. Telzey was shaking violently. It had been, she was telling herself, a deliberate test . . . not of herself, of course, but of TT. And Tick-Tock had passed with honors. That her nerves had been half ruined in the process would seem a matter of no consequence to this rugged crew. . . .

She realized next that someone here was addressing her personally.

It took a few moments to steady her jittering thoughts enough to gain a more definite impression than that. This speaker, she discovered then,

was a member of the circle of whom she hadn't
been aware before. The thought-impressions
came hard and cold as iron—it was a personage
who was very evidently in the habit of making
major decisions and seeing them carried out. The
circle, its moment of sport over, was listening
with more than a suggestion of deference. Tick-
Tock, far from conciliated, green eyes still blazing, nevertheless was settling down to listen too.

Telzey began to understand.

Her suggestions, Iron Thoughts informed her,
might appear without value to a number of
foolish minds here, but he intended to see they
were given a fair trial. Did he perhaps hear, he
inquired next of the circle, throwing in a casual
but horridly vivid impression of snapping spines
and slashed shaggy throats spouting blood, any
objection to that?

Dead stillness all around. There was, definitely, no objection! Tick-Tock began to grin like a
pleased kitten.

That point having been settled in an orderly
manner now, Iron Thoughts went on coldly to
Telzey, what specifically did she propose they
should do?

IV

HALET'S LONG, pearl-gray sportscar showed up
above the park trees twenty minutes later. Telzey, face turned down towards the open law library in her lap, watched the car from the corner
of her eyes. She was in plain view, sitting beside
the lake, apparently absorbed in legal research.
Tick-Tock, camouflaged among the bushes thirty
feet higher up the bank, had spotted the car an
instant before she did and announced the fact
with a three-second break in her purring. Neither
of them made any other move.

The car was approaching the lake but still a
good distance off. Its canopy was down, and Telzey could just make out the heads of three people
inside. Delquos, Halet's chauffeur, would be flying the vehicle, while Halet and Dr. Droon
looked around for her from the sides. Three
hundred yards away, the aircar began a turn to
the right. Delquos didn't like his employer much;
at a guess, he had just spotted Telzey and was
trying to warn her off.

Telzey closed the library and put it down,
picked up a handful of pebbles and began flicking them idly, one at a time, into the water. The
aircar vanished to her left.

Three minutes later, she watched its shadow
glide across the surface of the lake towards her.
Her heart began to thump almost audibly, but she

didn't look up. Tick-Tock's purring continued, on its regular, unhurried note. The car came to a stop almost directly overhead. After a couple of seconds, there was a clicking noise. The purring ended abruptly.

Telzey climbed to her feet as Delquos brought the car down to the bank of the lake. The chauffeur grinned ruefully at her. A side door had been opened, and Halet and Dr. Droon stood behind it. Halet watched Telzey with a small smile while the naturalist put the heavy life-detector-and-stungun device carefully down on the floorboards.

"If you're looking for Tick-Tock," Telzey said, "she isn't here."

Halet shook her head sorrowfully.

"There's no use lying to us dear! Dr. Droon just stunned her."

They found TT collapsed on her side among the shrubs, wearing her natural color. Her eyes were shut; her chest rose and fell in a slow breathing motion. Dr. Droon, looking rather apologetic, pointed out to Telzey that her pet was in no pain, that the stungun had simply put her comfortably to sleep. He also explained the use of the two sets of webbed paralysis belts which he fastened about TT's legs. The effect of the stun charge would wear off in a few minutes, and contact with the inner surfaces of the energized belts would then keep TT anesthetized and unable to move until the belts were removed. She would, he repeated, be suffering no pain through the process.

Telzey didn't comment. She watched Delquos raise TT's limp body above the level of the bushes with a gravity hoist belonging to Dr. Droon, and maneuver her back to the car, the others following. Delquos climbed into the car first, opened the big trunk compartment in the rear. TT was slid inside and the trunk compartment locked.

"Where are you taking her?" Telzey asked sullenly as Delquos lifted the car into the air.

"To the spaceport, dear," Halet said. "Dr. Droon and I both felt it would be better to spare your feelings by not prolonging the matter unnecessarily."

Telzey wrinkled her nose disdainfully, and walked up the aircar to stand behind Delquos's seat. She leaned against the back of the seat for an instant. Her legs felt shaky.

The chauffeur gave her a sober wink from the side.

"That's a dirty trick she's played on you, Miss Telzey!" he murmured. "I tried to warn you."

"I know." Telzey took a deep breath. "Look, Delquos, in just a minute something's going to happen! It'll look dangerous, but it won't be. Don't let it get you nervous . . . right?"

"Huh?" Delquos appeared startled, but kept his voice low. "Just *what's* going to happen?"

"No time to tell you. Remember what I said."

Telzey moved back a few steps from the driver's seat, turned around, said unsteadily, "Halet, Dr. Droon . . ."

Halet had been speaking quietly to Dr. Droon; they both looked up.

"If you don't move, and don't do anything stupid," Telzey said rapidly, "you won't get hurt. If you do . . . well, I don't know! You see, there's another crest cat in the car . . ." In her mind she added, "Now!"

It was impossible to tell in just what section of the car Iron Thoughts had been lurking. The carpeting near the rear passenger seats seemed to blur for an instant. Then he was there, camouflage dropped, sitting on the floorboards five feet from the naturalist and Halet.

Halet's mouth opened wide; she tried to scream but fainted instead. Dr. Droon's right hand started out quickly towards the big stungun device beside his seat. Then he checked himself and sat still, ashen-faced.

Telzey didn't blame him for changing his mind. She felt he must be a remarkably brave man to have moved at all. Iron Thoughts, twice as broad across the back as Tick-Tock, twice as massively muscled, looked like a devil-beast even to her. His dark-green marbled hide was criss-crossed with old scar patterns; half his toss-ing crimson chest appeared to have been ripped away. He reached out now in a fluid, silent mo-tion, hooked a paw under the stungun and flicked upwards. The big instrument rose in an incredi-bly swift, steep arc eighty feet into the air, various parts flying away from it, before it started curving down towards the treetops below the car. Iron Thoughts lazily swung his head around and looked at Telzey with yellow fire-eyes.

"Miss Telzey! Miss Telzey!" Delquos was mut-tering behind her. "You're sure it won't . . ."

Telzey swallowed. At the moment, she felt barely mouse-sized again. "Just relax!" she told

Delquos in a shaky voice. "He's really quite t-t-t-tame."

Iron Thoughts produced a harsh but not un-amiable chuckle in her mind.

The pearl-gray sportscar, covered now by its streamlining canopy, drifted down presently to a parking platform outside the suite of offices of Jontarou's Planetary Moderator, on the four-teenth floor of the Shikaris' Club Tower. An at-tendant waved it on into a vacant slot.

Inside the car, Delquos set the brakes, switched off the engine, asked, "Now what?"

"I think," Telzey said reflectively, "we'd better lock you in the trunk compartment with my aunt and Dr. Droon while I talk to the Moderator."

The chauffeur shrugged. He'd regained most of his aplomb during the unhurried trip across the parklands. Iron Thoughts had done nothing but sit in the center of the car, eyes half shut, looking like instant death, enjoying a dignified nap and occasionally emitting a ripsawing noise which might have been either his style of purring or a snore. And Tick-Tock, when Delquos peeled the paralysis belts off her legs at Telzey's direction, had greeted him with her usual reserved affabil-ity. What the chauffeur was suffering from at the moment was mainly intense curiosity, which Telzey had done nothing to relieve.

"Just as you say, Miss Telzey," he agreed. "I hate to miss whatever you're going to be doing here, but if you *don't* lock me up now, Miss Halet will figure I was helping you and fire me as soon as you let her out."

Telzey nodded, then cocked her head in the direction of the rear compartment. Faint sounds coming through the door indicated that Halet had regained consciousness and was having hysterics.

"You might tell her," Telzey suggested, "that there'll be a grown-up crest cat sitting outside the compartment door." This wasn't true, but neither Delquos nor Halet could know it. "If there's too much racket before I get back, it's likely to irritate him. . . ."

A minute later, she set both car doors on lock and went outside, wishing she were less informally clothed. Sunbriefs and sandals tended to make her look juvenile.

The parking attendant appeared startled when she approached him with Tick-Tock striding along beside her.

"They'll never let you into the offices with that thing, miss," he informed her. "Why, it doesn't even have a collar!"

"Don't worry about it," Telzey told him aloofly. She dropped a two-credit piece she'd taken from Halet's purse into his hand, and continued on towards the building entrance. The attendant squinted after her, trying unsuccessfully to dispel an odd impression that the big catlike animal with the girl was throwing a double shadow.

The Moderator's chief receptionist also had some doubts about TT, and possibly about the sunbriefs, though she seemed impressed when Telzey's identification tag informed her she was speaking to the daughter of Federation Councilwoman Jessamine Amberdon.

"You feel you can discuss this—emergency—

only with the Moderator himself, Miss Amberdon?" she repeated.

"Exactly," Telzey said firmly. A buzzer sounded as she spoke. The receptionist excused herself and picked up an earphone. She listened a moment, said blandly, "Yes. Of course. Yes, I understand," replaced the earphone and stood up, smiling at Telzey.

"Would you come with me, Miss Amberdon?" she said. "I think the Moderator will see you immediately."

Telzey followed her, chewing thoughtfully at her lip. This was easier than she'd expected—in fact, too easy! Halet's work? Probably. A few comments to the effect of "A highly imaginative child . . . overexcitable," while Halet was arranging to have the Moderator's office authorize Tick-Tock's transfer to the Life Banks, along with the implication that Jessamine Amberdon would appreciate a discreet handling of any disturbance Telzey might create as a result.

It was the sort of notion that would appeal to Halet. . . .

They passed through a series of elegantly equipped offices and hallways, Telzey grasping TT's neck-fur in lieu of a leash, their appearance creating a tactfully restrained wave of surprise among secretaries and clerks. And if somebody here and there was troubled by a fleeting, uncanny impression that not one large beast but two seemed to be trailing the Moderator's visitor down the aisles, no mention was made of what could have been only a momentary visual distortion. Finally, a pair of sliding doors opened ahead, and the receptionist ushered Telzey into a large, cool balcony garden on the shaded side of the great building. A tall, gray-haired man stood up from the desk at which he was working, and bowed to Telzey. The receptionist withdrew again.

"My pleasure, Miss Amberdon," Jontarou's Planetary Moderator said. "Be seated, please." He studied Tick-Tock with more than casual interest while Telzey was settling herself into a chair, added, "And what may I and my office do for you?"

Telzey hesitated. She'd observed his type on Orado in her mother's circle of acquaintances . . . a senior diplomat, a man not easy to impress. It was a safe bet that he'd had her brought out to his balcony office only to keep her occupied while Halet was quietly informed where the Amberdon problem child was and requested to come over and take charge.

What she had to tell him now would have sounded rather wild even if presented by a presumably responsible adult. She could provide proof, but until the Moderator was already nearly sold on her story, that would be a very unsafe thing to do. Old Iron Thoughts was backing her up, but if it didn't look as if her plans were likely to succeed, he would be willing to ride herd on his devil's pack just so long. . . .

Better start the ball rolling without any preliminaries, Telzey decided. The Moderator's picture of her must be that of a spoiled, neurotic brat in a stew about the threatened loss of a pet animal. He expected her to start arguing with him immediately about Tick-Tock.

She said, "Do you have a personal interest in

keeping the Baluit crest cats from becoming extinct?"

Surprise flickered in his eyes for an instant. Then he smiled.

"I admit I do, Miss Amberdon," he said pleasantly. "I should like to see the species reestablished. I count myself almost uniquely fortunate in having had the opportunity to bag two of the magnificent brutes before disease wiped them out on the planet."

The last seemed a less than fortunate statement just now. Telzey felt a sharp tingle of alarm, then sensed that in the minds which were drawing the meaning of the Moderator's speech from her mind there had been only a brief stir of interest.

She cleared her throat, said, "The point is that they weren't wiped out by disease."

He considered quizzically, seemed to wonder what she was trying to lead up to. Telzey gathered her courage, plunged on, "Would you like to hear what did happen?"

"I should be much interested, Miss Amberdon," the Moderator said without change of expression. "But first, if you'll excuse me a moment . . ."

There had been some signal from his desk which Telzey hadn't noticed, because he picked up a small communicator now, said, "Yes?" After a few seconds, he resumed, "That's rather curious, isn't it? Yes, I'd try that. No, that shouldn't be necessary. . . . Yes, please do. Thank you." He replaced the communicator, his face very sober; then, his eyes flicking for an instant to TT, he drew one of the upper desk drawers open a few inches, and turned back to Telzey.

"Now, Miss Amberdon," he said affably, "you were about to say? About these crest cats . . ."

Telzey swallowed. She hadn't heard the other side of the conversation, but she could guess what it had been about. His office had called the guest house, had been told by Halet's maid that Halet, the chauffeur and Dr. Droon were out looking for Miss Telzey and her pet. The Moderator's office had then checked on the sportscar's communication number and attempted to call it. And, of course, there had been no response.

To the Moderator, considering what Halet would have told him, it must add up to the grim possibility that the young lunatic he was talking to had let her three-quarters-grown crest cat slaughter her aunt and the two men when they caught up with her! The office would be notifying the police now to conduct an immediate search for the missing aircar.

When it would occur to them to look for it on the Moderator's parking terrace was something Telzey couldn't know. But if Halet and Dr. Droon were released before the Moderator accepted her own version of what had occurred, and the two reported the presence of wild crest cats in Port Nichay, there would be almost no possibility of keeping the situation under control. Somebody was bound to make some idiotic move, and the fat would be in the fire. . . .

Two things might be in her favor. The Moderator seemed to have the sort of steady nerve one would expect in a man who had bagged two Baluit crest cats. The partly opened desk drawer beside him must have a gun in it; apparently he considered that a sufficient precaution against an attack by TT. He wasn't likely to react in a panicky manner. And the mere fact that he suspected Telzey of homicidal tendencies would make him give the closest attention to what she said. Whether he believed her then was another matter, of course.

Slightly encouraged, Telzey began to talk. It did sound like a thoroughly wild story, but the Moderator listened with an appearance of intent interest. When she had told him as much as she felt he could be expected to swallow for a start, he said musingly, "So they weren't wiped out—they went into hiding! Do I understand you to say they did it to avoid being hunted?"

Telzey chewed her lip frowningly before replying. "There's something about that part I don't quite get," she admitted. "Of course, I don't quite get either why you'd want to go hunting . . . twice for something that's just as likely to bag you instead!"

"Well, those are, ah, merely the statistical odds." the Moderator explained. "If one has enough confidence, you see . . ."

"I don't really. But the crest cats seem to have felt the same way—at first. They were getting around one hunter for every cat that got shot. Humans were the most exciting game they'd ever run into.

"But then that ended, and the humans started knocking them out with stunguns from aircars where they couldn't be got at, and hauling them off while they were helpless. After it had gone on for a while, they decided to keep out of sight.

"But they're still around . . . thousands and thousands of them! Another thing nobody's known about them is that they weren't only in the Baluit mountains. There were crest cats scattered all through the big forests along the other side of the continent."

"Very interesting," the Moderator commented. "Very interesting, indeed!" He glanced towards the communicator, then returned his gaze to Telzey, drumming his fingers lightly on the desk top.

She could tell nothing at all from his expression now, but she guessed he was thinking hard. There was supposed to be no native intelligent life in the legal sense on Jontarou, and she had been careful to say nothing so far to make the Baluit cats look like more than rather exceptionally intelligent animals. The next—rather large —question should be how she'd come by such information.

If the Moderator asked her that, Telzey thought, she could feel she'd made a beginning at getting him to buy the whole story. . . .

"Well," he said abruptly, "if the crest cats are not extinct or threatened with extinction, the Life Banks obviously have no claim on your pet." He smiled confidingly at her. "And that's the reason you're here, isn't it?"

"Well, no," Telzey began, dismayed. "I . . ."

"Oh, it's quite all right, Miss Amberdon! I'll simply rescind the permit which was issued for the purpose. You need feel no further concern about that." He paused. "Now, just one question . . . do you happen to know where your aunt is at present?"

Telzey had a dead, sinking feeling. So he

hadn't believed a word she said. He'd been stalling her along until the aircar could be found.

She took a deep breath. "You'd better listen to the rest of it."

"Why, is there more?" the Moderator asked politely.

"Yes. The important part! The kind of creatures they are, they couldn't go into hiding indefinitely just because someone was after them."

Was there a flicker of something beyond watchfulness in his expression. "What would they do, Miss Amberdon?" he asked quietly.

"If they couldn't get at the men in the aircars and couldn't communicate with them"—the flicker again!—"they'd start looking for the place the men came from, wouldn't they? It might take them some years to work their way across the continent and locate us here in Port Nichay. But supposing they did it finally and a few thousand of them are sitting around in the parks down there right now? They could come up the side of these towers as easily as they go up the side of a mountain. And supposing they'd decided that the only way to handle the problem was to clean out the human beings in Port Nichay?"

The Moderator stared at her in silence a few seconds. "You're saying," he observed then, "that they're rational beings—above the Critical I.Q. level."

"Well," Telzey said, "legally they're rational. I checked on that. About as rational as we are, I suppose."

"And would you mind telling me how you happen to know these things?"

"They told me," Telzey said bluntly.

He was silent again, studying her face. "You mentioned, Miss Amberdon, that they have been unable to communicate with other human beings. This suggest then that you are a xenotelepath. . . ."

"I am?" Telzey hadn't heard the term before. "If it means that I can tell what the cats are thinking, and they can tell what I'm thinking, I guess that's the word for it." She considered him, decided she had him almost on the ropes, went on quickly. "I looked up the laws, and told them they could conclude a treaty with the Federation which would establish them as an Affiliated Species . . . and that would settle everything the way they would want it settled, without trouble. Some of them believed me. They decided to wait until I could talk to you. If it works out, fine! If it doesn't"—she felt her voice falter for an instant— "they're going to cut loose fast!"

The Moderator seemed undisturbed. "And what am I supposed to do?"

"I told them you'd contact the Council of the Federation on Orado."

"Contact the Council?" he repeated coolly. "With no more proof for this story than your word, Miss Amberdon?"

Telzey felt a quick, angry stirring begin about her, felt her face whiten.

"All right," she said. "I'll give you proof! I'll have to now. But that'll be it. Once they've tipped their hand all the way, you'll have about thirty seconds left to make the right move. I hope you remember that!"

He cleared his throat. "I . . ."

"NOW!" Telzey said.

Along the walls of the balcony garden, beside the ornamental flower stands, against the edges of the rock pool, the crest cats appeared. Perhaps thirty of them. None quite as physically impressive as Iron Thoughts who stood closest to the Moderator, but none very far from it. Motionless as rocks, frightening as gargoyles, they waited, eyes glowing with hellish excitement.

"This is their council, you see," Telzey heard herself saying. "The chiefs of the tribes . . ."

The Moderator's face had also paled. But he was, after all, an old shikari and a senior diplomat. He took an unhurried look around the circle, said quietly, "Accept my profound apologies for doubting you, Miss Amberdon!" and reached for the desk communicator.

Iron Thoughts swung his demon head in Telzey's direction. For an instant, she picked up the mental impression of a fierce yellow eye closing in an approving wink.

". . . an open transmitter line to Orado," the Moderator was saying into the communicator. "The Council. And snap it up! Some very important visitors are waiting. . . ."

The offices of Jontarou's Planetary Moderator became an extremely busy and interesting area then. Quite two hours passed before it occurred to anyone to ask Telzey again whether she knew where her aunt was at present.

Telzey smote her forehead.

"Forgot all about that!" she admitted, fishing the sportscar's keys out of the pocket of her sunbriefs. "They're out on the parking platform. . . ."

When the trunk compartment was opened, Delquos and Dr. Droon looked rather worn out. Halet was still having hysterics.

V

THE PRELIMINARY treaty arrangements between the Federation of the Hub and the new Affiliated Species of the Planet of Jontarou were formally ratified two weeks later, the ceremony taking place on Jontarou, in the Champagne Hall of the Shikaris' Club.

Telzey was able to follow the event only by news viewer in her ship-cabin, she and Halet being on the return trip to Orado by then. She wasn't too interested in the treaty's details—they conformed almost exactly to what she had read out to Iron Thoughts and his co-chiefs and companions in the park. It was the smooth bridging of the wide language gap between the contracting parties by a row of interpreting machines and a handful of human xenotelepaths which held her attention.

As she switched off the viewer, Halet came wandering in from the adjoining cabin.

"I was watching it too!" Halet observed. She smiled. "I was hoping to see dear Tick-Tock."

Telzey looked over at her. "Well, TT would hardly be likely to show up in Port Nichay," she said. "She's having too good a time now finding out what life in the Baluit range is like."

"I suppose so," Halet agreed doubtfully, sitting down on a hassock. "But I'm glad she promised to get in touch with us again in a few years. I'll miss her."

Telzey regarded her aunt with a reflective frown. Halet meant it quite sincerely, of course; she had undergone a profound change of heart during the past two weeks. But Telzey wasn't without some doubts about the actual value of a change of heart brought on by telepathic means. The learning process the crest cats had started in her mind appeared to have continued automatically several days longer than her rugged teachers had really intended; and Telzey had reason to believe that by the end of that time she'd developed associated latent abilities of which the crest cats had never heard. She'd barely begun to get it all sorted out yet, but, as an example, she'd found it remarkably easy to turn Halet's more obnoxious attitudes virtually upside down. It had taken her a couple of days to get the hang of her aunt's personal symbolism, but after that there had been no problem. The question remained whether it had been such a good thing to do.

She was reasonably certain she'd broken no laws so far, though the sections in the law library covering the use and abuse of psionic abilities were veiled in such intricate and downright obscuring phrasing—deliberately, Telzey suspected—that it was really difficult to say what they did mean. But even aside from that, there were a number of arguments in favor of exercising great caution.

Jessamine, for one thing, was bound to start worrying about her sister-in-law's health if Halet turned up on Orado in her present state of mind, even though it would make for a far more agreeable atmosphere in the Amberdon household. . . .

"Halet," Telzey inquired mentally, "do you remember what an all-out stinker you used to be?"

"Of course, dear," Halet said aloud. "I can hardly wait to tell dear Jessamine how much I regret the many times I—"

"Well," Telzey went on, still verbalizing it silently, "I think you'd really enjoy life more if you were, let's say, about halfway between your old nasty self and the sort of sickening-good kind you are now."

"Why, Telzey!" Halet cried out with dopey amiability. "What a delightful idea!"

"Let's try it," Telzey said.

There was silence in the cabin for some twenty minutes then while she went painstakingly about remolding a number of Halet's character traits for the second time. She still felt some misgivings about it; but if it became necessary, she probably could always restore the old Halet in toto.

These, she told herself, definitely were powers one should treat with respect! Better rattle through law school first; then, with that out of the way, she could start hunting around to see who in the Federation was qualified to instruct a genius-level novice in the proper handling of psionics. . . .

PART TWO

VI

At the Orado City Space Terminal, the Customs and Public Health machine was smoothly checking through passengers disembarking from a liner from Jontarou. A psionic computer of awesome dimensions, the machine formed one side of a great hall along which the stream of travelers moved towards the city exits and their previously cleared luggage. Unseen behind the base of the wall—armored, as were the housing of all Federation psionic machines in public use—its technicians sat in rows of cubicles, eyes fixed on dials and indicators, hands ready to throw pinpointing switches at the quiver of a blip.

The computer's sensors were simultaneously searching for contraband and dutiable articles, and confirming the medical clearance given passengers before an interstellar ship reached Orado's atmosphere. Suggestions of inimical or unregistered organisms, dormant or active, would be a signal to quarantine-attendants, at the end of the slideways, to shepherd somebody politely to a detention ward for further examination. Customs agents were waiting for the other type of signal.

It was a dependable, unobtrusive procedure, causing no unnecessary inconvenience or delay, and so generally established now at major spaceports in the Federation of the Hub that sophisticated travelers simply took it for granted. However, the machine had features of which neither Customs nor Health were aware. In a room across the spaceport, two men sat watchfully before another set of instruments connected to the computer's scanners. Above these instruments was a wide teleview of the Customs hall. Nothing appeared to be happening in the room until approximately a third of the passengers from Jontarou had moved through the computer's field. Then the instruments were suddenly active, and a personality identification chart popped out of a table slot before the man on the left.

He glanced at the chart, said, "Telzey Amberdon. It's our pigeon. Fix on her!"

The man on the right grunted, eyes on the screen where the teleview pickup had shifted abruptly to a point a few yards ahead of and above a girl who had just walked into the hall. Smartly dressed and carrying a small handbag, she was a slim and dewy teenager, tanned, blue-eyed, and brown-haired. As the pickup began to move along the slideway with her, the man on the right closed a switch, placed his hand on a plunger.

Simultaneously, two things occurred in the hall. Along the ceiling a string of nearly microscopic ports opened, extruding needle paralyzers pointed at the girl; and one of the floating ambulances moored tactfully out of sight near the exits rose, shifted forward twenty feet and stopped again. If the girl collapsed, she would be on her way out of the hall in a matter of seconds, the event almost unnoticed except by the passengers nearest her.

"If you want her, we have her," said the man on the right.

"We'll see." The first observer slipped the identification chart into one of his instruments, and slowly depressed a calibrated stud, watching the girl's face in the teleview.

Surprise briefly widened her eyes; then her expression changed to sharp interest. After a moment, the observer experienced a sense of question in himself, an alert, searching feeling.

Words abruptly formed in his mind.

"Is somebody there? Did somebody speak just now?"

The man on the right grinned.

"A lamb!"

"Maybe." The first observer looked thoughtful. "Don't relax just yet. The response was Class Two."

He waited while the sense of question lingered, strengthened for a few seconds, then faded. He selected a second stud on the instrument, edged it down.

This time, the girl's mobile features showed no reaction, and nothing touched his mind. The observer shifted his eyes to a dial pointer, upright and unmoving before him, watched it while a minute ticked past, released the stud. Sliding the identification pattern chart out of the instrument, he checked over the new factors coded into it, and returned it to the table slot.

Forty-two miles off in Orado City, in the headquarters complex of the Federation's Psychology Service, another slot opened, and the chart slid out on a desk. Somebody picked it up.

"Hooked and tagged and never knew it," the
first observer was remarking. "You can call off
the fix." He reached for a cigarette, added, "Fifteen years old. She was spotted for the first time
two weeks ago. . . ."

In the Customs hall the tiny ports along the
ceiling sealed themselves and the waiting ambu-
lance slid slowly back to its mooring points.

The visiting high Federation official was
speaking in guardedly even tones.

"I, as has everyone else," he said, "have been
led to believe that the inspection machine provided by the Psychology Service for Health and
Customs respected the anonymity of the public."

He paused. "Obviously, this can't be recon-
ciled with the ability—displayed just now—of
identifying individuals by their coded charts!"

Boddo, director of the Psychology Service's
Department Eighty-four, laid the identification
chart marked with the name of Telzey Amberdon
down before him. He looked at it for a moment
without speaking, his long, bony face and
slanted thick brows giving him a somewhat
satanic appearance. The visitor recently had
been appointed to a Federation position which
made it necessary to provide him with ordinarily
unavailable information regarding the Psychology Service's means and methods of operation.
He had spent two days being provided with it, in
department after department of the Service, and
was showing symptoms, not unusual on such
occasions, of accumulated shock.

The policy in these cases was based on the

assumption that the visitor possessed considerable intelligence, or he would not have been there. He should be given ample time to work out the shock and revise various established opinions. If he failed to do this, his mind would be delicately doctored before he left Headquarters, with the result that he would forget most of what he had learned and presently discover good reason for taking another job—specifically one which did not involve intimate contacts with the Psychology Service.

Boddo, not an unkind man, decided to do what he could to help this unwitting probationer over the hump.

"The Customs computer isn't supposed to be able to identify individuals," he agreed. "But I believe you already know that many of the psionic machines we put out aren't limited to the obvious functions they perform."

"Yes, I have learned that! I understand, of course, that complete candor can't always be demanded of a government agency." With an impatient wave of his arm, the visitor indicated the one-way screen through which they had looked in on the room at the spaceport. "But this is deliberate, planned deception! And more than that. If I understood correctly what happened just now, the so-called Customs machine—supposedly there simply to expedite traffic and safeguard the health of this world—not only identifies unsuspecting persons for you but actually reads their minds!"

"The last to a rather limited extent," Boddo said. "It's far from being the best all-around device for that purpose."

"Be that as it may! The presence of such a machine at the spaceport constitutes a violation of the public's right to privacy of thought."

"Of course, it does," Boddo said. "In practice a vanishingly small fraction of the public is affected. I couldn't care less about having the thoughts of the average man or woman invaded; and if I wanted to, I wouldn't have the time. Department Eighty-four is the branch of the Service's intelligence which investigates, registers, records and reports on psis, and real or apparent psionic manifestations outside the Service. This office co-ordinates such information. We aren't interested in anything else."

The visitor stared at him, face flushed, scowling undecidedly. It would be best to have him let off a little more steam before taking up the business for which he had been sent here. "I imagine," Boddo suggested, "you've been told of the overall program to have advanced psionic machines in general use throughout the Hub in the not too distant future?"

The official reddened further. "A monstrously expensive and wasteful project, sir! But that isn't my concern. What appalls me are the dangers to the public that are inherent in such a plan."

Boddo thoughtfully cleared his throat.

"The clandestine uses to which these machines are being put today," the visitor went on, "certainly are undesirable enough. The fact that this practice apparently is condoned at the highest levels of Federation government does not make it any less disturbing! To the contrary. What is to insure that the further spread of your devices won't lead to the transformation of the

Federation into a police state with an utterly unbreakable hold on the minds of the population? The temptation ... the possibility ... will always be there."

Boddo thoughtfully cleared his throat.

The official stabbed an accusing finger at him.

"But if that does not happen," he said, "if instead the reckless plan to turn these instruments over in great numbers—and within a few decades—to virtually anyone who happens to want them actually is carried out, the situation will be as bad, or worse. Inevitably, the machine will multiply the tremendous problems already presented by organized crime, by power politics, by greed, stupidity and ignorance. Our civilization, sir, simply has not matured to the point where powers of that nature should be entrusted to it! The most disastrous abuses must follow as a matter of course."

"Well," Boddo said, "you realize I'm not a policy maker. I'm not really qualified to argue such questions with you. Of course, the fact that the program has, as you remarked, the approval of the highest level of Federation government indicates that the reasoning behind it isn't entirely unsound. As I've understood it, the gradual, orderly introduction of psionic machines is expected to solve the problems you've mentioned progressively as the program unfolds. When you have the complete picture on that, you may find your opinions changing."

The visitor's mouth tightened.

"The functions of a number of the Service's other departments already have been explained to me," he remarked. "I've heard nothing so far to cause me to change my opinion. As for your own office—the control of the so-called human psis—I may as well tell you frankly what I think of it."

"Please do," Boddo said.

The official smiled coldly. "You're engaged in a witch hunt, my dear sirs! Psionics is a sensitive subject nowadays. I'm not uninformed about the potentialities of dowsers, professional mind-readers, fortune-tellers, and the like. Their tricks are interesting, and may be useful, but have no real significance. However, a clever campaign to divert the public's concern to such people might very well leave the psionic machines looking very innocuous by comparison."

"Um . . ." Boddo pursed his lips, frowning. "As it happens," he observed, "the purpose of this office is almost the reverse of what you suggest."

"I don't follow that," the visitor said shortly.

Boddo said, "You are not in possession of sufficient facts in that area. That, of course, is why you're here at the moment. I'm to supply you with facts. And to start with, I'll say that the last thing in the world we'd want is to bring the information this office gathers to the public's attention. The Service, of course, is conducting a continuous campaign on many fronts to reduce uneasiness and hostility about psionic machines. Our specific assignment is to prevent occurrences—arising from the activities of human psis—which might strengthen that feeling. Or, if they can't be prevented, to provide harmless explanations for them, and to make sure they aren't repeated—at least not by the psi in question."

The official scowled. "I still don't see . . . What occurrences?"

"We are not," Boddo said patiently, "in the least worried about what dowsers, professional mind-readers and fortune-tellers might do. Not at all. The public's familiar with them and regards them on the whole as harmlessly freakish. When the performance of such a person is sufficiently dependable, we call him or her a Class One psi. Class One falls into rather neat categories— eighteen, to be exact—and functions in a stereotyped manner. The Class One, in fact, is almost defined by his limitations."

"Then . . ."

"Yes," Boddo said, "there's another type. The Class Two. A rare bird, as he apparently always has been. But recent breakthroughs in psionic theory and practice make it easier to identify him. We feel that the most desirable place for a Class Two at present is in the Psychology Service. I'll introduce you presently to a few of them."

"I . . . what kind of people are they?"

Boddo shrugged. "Not too remarkable—except for their talents. If you met the average Class Two, you'd see a normal, perhaps somewhat unusually healthy human being. As for the talents, anything a Class One can do, the Class Two who has developed the same line does better; and he's almost never restricted to a specialty, or even to two or three specialties. In that respect, his talent corresponds more closely to normal human faculties and acquired skills. It can be explored, directed, trained and developed."

"Developed to what extent?" the official asked.

"It depends on the individual. You mentioned mind-reading. In the Class Two who has the faculty, it may appear as anything from a Class One's general impressions or sensing of scattered specific details on up. Up to the almost literal reading of minds." Boddo looked thoughtfully at the visitor. "A very few can tell what's passing through any mind they direct their attention on as readily and accurately as if they were reading a tape. The existence of such people is one of the things we prefer not to have publicized at present. It might produce unfavorable reactions."

Doubt and uneasiness were showing in the visitor's face. "That would not be surprising. Such abnormal powers leave the ordinary man at a severe disadvantage."

"True enough," Boddo said. "But the ordinary man is under a similar disadvantage whenever he confronts someone who is considerably more intelligent or more experienced than himself, or who simply points a gun at him. And he's much more likely to run into difficulties like that. It's extremely improbable that he would come to the attention of a capable Class Two mind-reader even once in his lifetime. If he did, the probability is again that the mind-reader would have no interest in him. But if he did happen to take an interest in our ordinary man, there's still no reason to assume it would be for any malevolent purpose."

The visitor cleared his throat. "But there are criminal psis?"

"Of course there are," Boddo said. "As a group, they show all normal human motivations, including the criminal ones. The Class Two tends to be a rather well-balanced individual, but we have compiled a sizable list of those who put their abilities to criminal use."

"And your office takes steps to protect the public against them?"

Boddo shook his head.

"Don't misunderstand me," he said. "It isn't my business to look out for the public. I believe you know that the only category of crimes with which the Psychology Service concerns itself directly are those against the Federation or against humanity. That applies also where psis are involved. What a Class Two does becomes of interest to us only when it might have an adverse effect on the psionic program. Then it doesn't matter whether he's actually committing crimes or not. We close down on him very quickly. Indirectly, of course; that does protect the public.

"Ordinarily, it isn't a question of malice. A Class Two may get careless, or he begins to engage in horse play at the expense of his neighbors. He's amusing himself. But as a result, he draws attention. Bizarre things have happened which seemingly can't be explained by ordinary reasoning. At other times, such incidents would cause some speculation and then be generally forgotten. At present, they can have more serious repercussions. So we try to prevent them. If necessary, we provide cover explanations and do what is necessary to bring the offending psi under control."

"In what way do you control these people?" the visitor asked.

Boddo picked up the personal identification chart of Telzey Amberdon.

"Let's consider the case of the young psi who came through the space terminal a short while ago," he said. "It will illustrate our general methods satisfactorily." He blinked at the codings on the chart for a moment, turned it over, thrust one end into a small glowing desk receptacle marked *For Occasional Observation*, withdrew it and dropped it into a filing slot.

"We knew this psi would be arriving on Orado today," he went on. "We'd had no previous contact with her, and only one earlier report which indicated she had acted as an xenotelepath—that is, she had been in mental communication with members of a telepathic nonhuman race. That particular ability appears in a relatively small number of psis, but its possessor is more often than not a Class One who fails to develop any associated talents.

"The check made at the spaceport showed immediately that this youngster is not Class One. She is beginning to learn to read human minds, with limitations perhaps due chiefly to a lack of experience, and she has discovered the art of telephypnosis, which is a misnamed process quite unrelated to ordinary hypnotic methods, though it produces similar general effects. These developments have all taken place within the past few weeks."

The visitor gave him a startled look. "You make that child sound rather dangerous!"

Boddo shrugged. "As far as this office is concerned, she is at present simply a Class Two, with a quite good though still largely latent potential. She picked up a scrambled telepathic impulse directed deliberately at her, but was not aware then that her mind was being scanned by our machine. A really accomplished Class Two would sense that. Neither did she realize that the machine was planting a compulsion in her mind."

"A compulsion?" the official repeated.

Boddo considered, said, "In effect, she's now provided with an artificial conscience regarding her paranormal talents which suggests, among other things, that she should seek proper authorization in using them. That's the standard procedure we follow after identifying a Class Two."

"It prevents them from using their abilities?"

"Not necessarily. It does tend to keep them out of minor mischief, but if they're sufficiently self-willed and motivated, they're quite likely to override the compulsion. That's particularly true if they discover what's happened, as some of them do. Still, it places a degree of restraint on them, and eventually leads a good number to the Psychology Serivice . . . which, of course, is what we want."

The visitor reflected. "What would you have done if the girl had realized the Customs machine was investigating her mind?"

Boddo smiled briefly. "Depending on her reactions, the procedure might have become a little more involved at that point. The ultimate result would have been about the same—the compulsion would have been installed."

"Why not simply invite the Class Two psis you discover to join the Service?"

Boddo shook his head. "If they refused, the invitation would have told them more about the Service than they should know while they remain at large. We rarely invite them unless we're prepared to use forcible means of induction if necessary. A satisfactory percentage show up of their own accord."

"What do you do about the others?"

"After they're identified and classed, it depends largely on what they do. Ordinarily, an occasional check is made of their activities. If they don't make a problem of themselves or show some development which requires closer study, we leave them alone."

There was a pause. The official looked thoughtful. He said finally, "You feel then that the Service's method of supervising psis is adequate?"

"It appears to keep the Class Two psis from causing trouble well enough," Boddo said. "Naturally, it isn't completely effective. For one thing, we can't expect to get a record of all of them. Then there's a divergent group called the unpredictables. Essentially they're just that. You might say the one thing they show in common is a highly erratic development of psionic ability."

"What do you do about them?"

Boddo said, "We have no formula for handling unpredictables. It wouldn't be worth the trouble to try to devise one which was flexible enough to meet every possibility. They're very rarely encountered."

"So rarely that there's no reason to worry about them?"

Boddo scratched his cheek, observed, "The Service doesn't regard an unpredictable as a cause for serious concern."

VII

Scowling with concentration, Telzey Amberdon sat, eyes closed, knees drawn up and arms locked about them, on the couch-bed in her side of duplex bungalow 18-19, Student Court Ninety-two, of Pehanron College. When she'd looked over at the rose-glowing pointers of a wall clock on the opposite side of the room, they had told her there wasn't much more than an hour left before Orado's sun would rise. That meant she had been awake all night, though she was only now beginning to feel waves of drowsiness.

Except for the glow from the clock, the room was dark, its windows shielded. She had thought of turning on lights, but there was a chance that a spot check by the college's automatic monitors would record the fact; and then Miss Eulate, the Senior Counselor of Section Ninety-two, was likely to show up during the morning to remind Telzey that a fifteen-year-old girl, even if she happened to be a privileged Star Honor Student, simply must get in her full and regular sleep periods.

It would be inconvenient just now if such an admonishment was accompanied by a suspension of honor student privileges. So the lights stayed out. Light, after all, wasn't a requirement in sitting there and probing about in an unsuspecting fellow-creature's mind, which was what Telzey had been engaged in during the night.

If the mind being probed had known what was going on, it might have agreed with Miss Eulate. But it didn't. It was the mind of a very large dog named Chomir, owned by Gonwil Lodis who occupied the other side of the duplex and was Telzey's best college friend, though her senior by almost four years.

Both Gonwil and Chomir were asleep, but Chomir slept fitfully. He was not given to prolonged concentration on any one subject, and for hours Telzey had kept him wearily half dreaming, over and over, about certain disturbing events which he hadn't really grasped when they occurred. He passed most of the night in a state of vague irritation, though his inquisitor was careful not to let the feeling become acute enough to bring him awake.

It wasn't pleasant for Telzey either. Investigating that section of Chomir's mind resembled plodding about in a dark swamp agitated by violent convulsions and covered by a smothering fog. From time to time, it became downright nerve-wracking as blasts of bewildered fury were transmitted to her with firsthand vividness out of the animal's memories. The frustrating side of it, however, was that the specific bits of information for which she searched remained obscured by the blurry, sporadic, nightmarish reliving which seemed to be the only form in which those memories could be made to show up just now. And it was extremely important to get the information because she suspected Chomir's experiences might mean that somebody was planning the deliberate murder of Gonwil Lodis.

She had got into the investigation almost by accident. Gonwil was one of the very few persons to whom Telzey had mentioned anything about her recently acquired ability to pry into other minds, and she had been on a walk with Chomir in the wooded hills above Pehanron College during the afternoon. Without apparent cause, Chomir suddenly had become angry, stared and sniffed about for a moment, then plunged bristling and snarling into the bushes. His mistress sprinted after him in high alarm, calling out a warning to anyone within earshot, because Chomir, though ordinarily a very well-mannered beast, was physically capable of taking a human being or somebody else's pet dog apart in extremely short order. But she caught up with him within a few hundred yards and discovered that his anger appeared to have spent itself as quickly as it had developed. Instead, he was acting now in an oddly confused and worried manner.

Gonwil thought he might have scented a wild animal. But his behavior remained a puzzle— Chomir had always treated any form of local wildlife they encountered as being beneath his notice. Half seriously, since she wasn't entirely convinced of Telzey's mind-reading ability, Gonwil suggested she might use it to find out what had disturbed him; and Telzey promised to try it after lights-out when Chomir had settled down to sleep. It would be her first attempt to study a canine mind, and it might be interesting.

Chomir turned out to be readily accessible to a probe, much more so than the half-dozen non-

telepathic human minds Telzey had looked into
so far, where many preliminary hours of search
had been needed to pick up an individual's
thought patterns and get latched solidly into
them. With Chomir she was there in around
thirty minutes. For a while, most of what she
encountered appeared grotesquely distorted and
incomprehensible; then something like a translating machine in Telzey's brain, which was the
xenotelepathic ability, suddenly clicked in, and
she found herself beginning to change the dog's
sleep impressions into terms which had a definite meaning to her. It was a little like discover-
ing the key to the operation of an unfamiliar
machine. She spent an hour investigating and
experimenting with a number of its mechanisms;
then, deciding she could control Chomir satisfactorily for her purpose, she shifted his thoughts in
the direction of what had happened that afternoon.

Around an hour or so later again, she stopped
to give them both a rest.

The event in the hills didn't look any less mys-
tifying now, but it had begun to acquire definitely sinister overtones. If Chomir had known of
the concept of unreality, he might have applied it
to what had occurred. He had realized suddenly
and with a blaze of rage that somewhere nearby
was a man whom he remembered from a previous meeting as representing a great danger to
Gonwil. He had rushed into the woods with
every intention of tearing off the man's head, but
then the fellow suddenly was gone again.

That was what had left Chomir in a muddled
and apprehensive frame of mind. The man had

both been there, and somehow not been there. Chomir felt approximately as a human being might have felt after an encounter with a menacing phantom which faded into thin air almost as soon as it was noticed. Telzey then tried to bring the earlier meeting with the mysterious stranger into view; but here she ran into so much confusion and fury that she got no clear details. There were occasional impressions of white walls—perhaps a large, white-walled room—and of a narrow-faced man, who somehow managed to stay beyond the reach of Chomir's teeth.

By that time, Telzey felt somewhat disturbed. Something out of the ordinary clearly had happened. And supposing the narrow-faced stranger did spell danger to Gonwil . . .

Gonwil had told her, laughing, not believing a word of it, a story she'd been hearing herself since she was a child; how on Tayun, the planet from which she had come to Orado to be a student at Pehanron, there were people who had been responsible for the death of her parents when she was less than a year old, and who intended eventually to kill Gonwil as the final act of revenge for some wrong her father supposedly had done.

Tayun appeared to have a well-established vendetta tradition, so the story might not be completely impossible. But as Gonwil told it, it did seem very unlikely.

On the other hand, who else could have any possible reason for wanting to harm Gonwil?

The instant she asked herself the question, Telzey felt a flick of alarmed shock. Because now that the possibility had occurred to her, she could answer the question immediately. She knew a group of people who might very well want to harm Gonwil, not as an act of vendetta but for the simple and logical reason that it would be very much to their material benefit if Gonwil died within the next few months.

She sat still a while, barely retaining her contacts with Chomir while she turned the thought around, considered it and let it develop. If she was right, this was an extremely ugly thing, and she could see nothing to indicate she was wrong.

Late last summer she had been invited to spend a few days with Gonwil as house guests of a lady who was Gonwil's closest living relative and a very dear friend, and who would be on Orado with her family for a short stay before returning to Tayun. Socially speaking, the visit was not a complete success, though Gonwil remained unaware of it. Telzey and the Parlin family—father, mother, and son—formed strong feeling of mutual dislike almost at sight, but stayed polite about it. Malrue Parlin was a handsome, energetic woman, who completely overshadowed her husband and son. She'd been almost excessively affectionate towards Gonwil.

It was Malrue, from what Telzey had heard, who had always been deeply concerned that the hypothetical vendettists might catch up with Gonwil some day. . . .

When his parents left, Parlin Junior remained on Orado with the avowed intention of winning Gonwil over to the idea of becoming his bride. Gonwil, though moderately fond of Junior, didn't care for the idea. But, more from fear of hurting Malrue's feelings than his, she'd been unable to bring herself to brush Junior off with sufficient firmness. At least, he'd kept returning.

And the thing, Telzey thought, it never had occurred to Gonwil, or to her, to speculate about was that Gonwil had inherited a huge financial fortune which Malrue Parlin was effectively controlling at present, and which she would go on controlling if Junior's suit was successful . . . or again if Gonwil happened to die before she came of age, which she would in just three months time.

In spite of Gonwil's diffidence in handling Junior, it must have become clear to both Junior and his mother some while ago that the marriage plan had fizzled.

One somehow didn't consider that people one had met, even if one hadn't liked them, might be planning murder. It seemed too unnatural. But murder was in fact the most common of major crimes anywhere in the Hub, and it was general knowledge that the more sophisticated murderers quite regularly escaped retribution. The Federation's legal code made no more than a gesture of attempting to cope with them. It was a structure of compromises in everything but its essentials, with the primary purpose of keeping six hundred billion human beings living in more than a thousand semi-autonomous sun systems away from wholesale conflicts, while the area of generally accepted lawful procedure and precedent was slowly but steadily extended. In that, it was surprisingly effective. But meanwhile individual citizens could suddenly find themselves in situations where Federation Law told them in effect that it could do nothing and advised them to look out for themselves.

Murder, aside from its more primitive forms, frequently provided such a situation. There was a legal term for it, with a number of semilegal implications. It was "private war."

Telzey's impulse was to wake up Gonwil and tell her what had occurred to her. But she rejected the idea. She had only her report of Chomir's experiences to add to things Gonwil already knew; and so far those experiences proved nothing even if Gonwil didn't assume they existed in Telzey's imagination rather than in Chomir's memory. She would be incapable of accepting, even theoretically, that Malrue might want her dead; and in attempting to disprove it, she might very well do something that would precipitate the danger.

The thing to go for first was more convincing evidence of danger. Telzey returned her attention to Chomir.

Near morning, she acknowledged to herself she would get no farther with the dog. He was responding more and more sluggishly and vaguely to her prods. She'd caught glimpses enough meanwhile to know his memory did hold evidence that wickedness of some kind was being brewed, but that was all. The animal mind couldn't co-operate any longer.

She should let Chomir rest for some hours at least. After he was fresh again, she might get at what she wanted without much trouble.

She eased off her contacts with his mind, drew away from it, felt it fade from her awareness. She opened her eyes again, yawned, sighed, reached over to the end of the couch and poked at the window control shielding. The room's windows appeared in the far wall, the shrubbery of the tiny bungalow garden swaying softly in the predawn quiet of the student court. Telzey turned bleary eyes towards the wall clock.

In an hour and a half, her father would be at his office in Orado City. The city was just under an hour away by aircar, and she'd have to get his advice and assistance in this matter at once. If Gonwil's death was planned, the time set for it probably wasn't many days away. Malrue and her husband were supposed to be on their way back to Orado for another of their annual visits, and Chomir's hated acquaintance had turned up again yesterday. The danger period could be expected to begin with Malrue's arrival.

By the time she'd showered, dressed and breakfasted, she found herself waking up again. Sunshine had begun to edge into the court. Telzey glanced at her watch, slipped on a wrist-talker, clipped her scintillating Star Honor Student pass to her hat, and poked at the duplex's interphone buzzer.

After some seconds, Gonwil's voice came drowsily from the instrument. "Uh . . . who . . ."

"Me."

"Oh . . . Whyya up so early?"

"It's broad daylight," Telzey said. "Listen, I'm flying in to Orado City to see my father. I'm starting right now. If anyone is interested, tell them I'll be back for lunch, or I'll call in."

"Right." Gonwil yawned audibly.

"I was wondering," Telzey went on. "When

did you say Mr. and Mrs. Parlin are due to land?"

"Day after tomorrow ... last I heard from Junior. Why?"

"Got anything planned for the first part of the holidays?"

"Well, just to stay away from Sonny somehow. He heard about the holidays."

"I've thought of something that will do it," Telzey said.

"Fine!" Gonwil said heartily. "What?"

"Tell you when I get back. You're free to leave after lunch, aren't you?"

Gonwil clucked doubtfully. "There's six more test tapes I'll have to clean up, and Finance Eleven is a living stinker! I think I can do it. I'll get at it right away. . . . Hey, wait a minute! Did you find out anything about . . . uh, well, yesterday?"

"We're started on it," Telzey said. "But I didn't really find out much."

In the carport back of the duplex, she eased herself into the driver's seat of a tiny Cloudsplitter and turned it into an enclosed ground traffic lane. The Star Honor Student pass got her through one of Pehanron's guard-screen exits without question; and a minute later the little car was airborne, streaking off towards the east.

Twenty miles on, Telzey checked the time again, set the Cloudsplitter to home in on one of Orado City's major traffic arteries, and released its controls. Her father should be about ready to leave his hotel by now. She dialed his call number on the car's communicator and tapped in her personal symbol.

Gilas Amberdon responded promptly. He had been, he acknowledged, about ready to leave;

and yes, he would be happy to see her at his office in around forty-five minutes. What was it about?

"Something to do with xenotelepathy," Telzey said.

"Let's hear it." His voice had changed tone slightly.

"That would take a little time, Gilas."

"I can spare the time."

He listened without comment while she told him about her attempt to explore Chomir's memories, what she seemed to have found, and what she was concluding from it. It would be easy to persuade Gonwil to keep out of sight for a day or two, with the idea of avoiding Junior; after that, her loyalty to Malrue might create additional problems.

Gilas remained silent for a little after she finished. Then he said, "I'll do two things immediately, Telzey."

"Yes?"

"I'll have the Kyth Agency send over an operator to discuss the matter—Dasinger, if he's available. If your mysterious stranger is remaining in the vicinity of Pehanron College, the agency should be able to establish who he is and what he's up to. Finding him might not be the most important thing, of course."

Telzey felt a surge of relief. "You do think Malrue Parlin . . ."

"We should have some idea about that rather soon. The fact is simply that if the situation between Gonwil and the Parlins is as you've described it in respect to the disposal of her holdings in case of death, it demands a close investigation in itself. Mrs. Parlin, while she isn't in the big leagues yet, is considered one of the sharper financial operators on Tayun."

"Gonwil says she's really brilliant."

"She might be," Gilas said. "In any case, we'll have a check started to determine whether there have been previous suggestions of criminality connected with her operations. We'll act meanwhile on the assumption that the danger exists and is imminent. Your thought of getting Gonwil away from the college for a couple of days, or until we see the situation more clearly, is a very good one. We'll discuss it when you get here."

"All right."

"I don't quite see," Gilas went on, "how we're going to explain what we want done, in the matter of the man the dog's run into twice, without revealing something of your methods of investigation."

"No. I thought of that."

He hesitated. "Well, Dasinger's agency is commendably close-mouthed about its clients' affairs. The information shouldn't go any farther. Are you coming in your own car?"

"Yes."

"Set it down on my private flange then. Ravia will take you through to the office."

VIII

Switching off the communicator, Telzey glanced at her watch. For the next thirty minutes, the Cloudsplitter would continue on automatic towards one of the ingoing Orado City air lanes. After it swung into the lane, she would make better time by taking over the controls. Meanwhile, she could catch up on some of the sleep she'd lost.

She settled back comfortably in the driver's seat and closed her eyes.

At once a figure which gave the impression of hugeness began to appear in her mind. Telzey flinched irritably. It had been over a week since the Psionic Cop last came climbing out of her unconscious to lecture her; she'd begun to hope she was finally rid of him. But he was back, a giant with a stern metallic face, looking halfway between one of the less friendly Orado City air patrolmen and the humanized type of robot. In a moment, he'd start warning her again that she was engaging in activities which could lead only to serious trouble. . . .

She opened her eyes abruptly and the Cop was gone. But she might as well give up the idea of a nap just now. The compulsion against using telepathy somebody had thoughtfully stuck her with was weakening progressively; but the long session with Chomir could have stirred it up enough to produce another series of nightmares in which the Psionic Cop chased her around to place her under arrest. Half an hour of nightmares wouldn't leave her refreshed for the meeting with Gilas's detectives.

Telzey straightened up, sat frowning at the horizon. There had been no way of foreseeing complications like the Psionic Cop when the telepathic natives of Jontarou nudged her dormant talent into action, a little over eight weeks ago. The prospects of life as a psi had looked rather intriguing. But hardly had she stepped out of the ship at Orado City when her problems began.

First, there'd been the touch of something very much like a strong other-mind impulse in the Customs Hall. Some seconds after it faded, Telzey realized it hadn't been structured enough to be some other telepath's purposeful thought. But she'd had no immediate suspicions. The Customs people used a psionically powered inspection machine, and she was within its field at the moment. Undoubtedly, she'd picked up a brief burst of meaningless psionic noise coming from the machine.

She forgot about that incident then, because her mother met her at the spaceport. Federation Councilwoman Jessamine Amberdon had been informed of the events on Jontarou, and appeared somewhat agitated about them. Telzey found herself whisked off promptly to be put through a series of psychological tests, to make sure she had come to no harm. Only when the tests indicated no alarming changes in her mental condition, in fact no detectable changes at all, did Jessamine seem reassured.

"Your father took immediate steps to have your part in the Jontarou matter hushed up," she informed Telzey. "And . . . well, xenotelepathy hardly seems very important! You're not too likely to run into telepathic aliens again." She smiled. "I admit I've been worried, but it seems no harm has been done. We can just forget the whole business now."

Telzey wasn't too surprised. Jessamine was a sweet and understanding woman, but she had the streak of conservatism which tended to characterize junior members of the Grand Council of the Federation. And discreet opinion-sampling on shipboard already had told Telzey that conservative levels of Hub society regarded skills like telepathy as being in questionable taste, if indeed, they were not simply a popular fiction. Jessamine must feel it could do nothing to further the brilliant career she foresaw for her daughter if it was rumored that Telzey had become a freak.

It clearly was not the right time to admit that additional talents of the kind had begun to burgeon in her on the trip home. Jessamine was due to depart from Orado with the Federation's austere Hace Committee within a few days, and might be absent for several months. It wouldn't do to get her upset all over again.

With Telzey's father, it was a different matter. Gilas Amberdon, executive officer of Orado City's Bank of Rienne, could, when he chose, adopt a manner conservative enough to make the entire Hace Committee look frivolous. But this had never fooled his daughter much, and Gilas didn't disappoint her.

"You appear," he observed in the course of their first private talk after her return, "to have grasped the principle that it rarely pays to give the impression of being too unusual."

"It looks that way," Telzey admitted.

"And of course," Gilas continued, "if one does happen to be quite unusual, there might eventually be positive advantages to having played the thing down."

"Yes," Telzey agreed. "I've thought of that."

Gilas tilted his chair back and laced his fingers behind his neck. It was his customary lecture position, though there appeared to be no lecture impending at the moment.

"What are your plans?" he asked.

"I want to finish law school first," Telzey said. "I think I can be out of Pehanron in about two years—but not if I get too involved in something else."

He nodded. "Then?"

"Then I might study telepathy and psionics generally. It looks as if it could be very interesting."

"Not a bad program," Gilas observed absently. He brought his chair back down to the floor, reached for a cigarette and lit it, eyes reflective.

"Psionics," he stated, "is a subject of which I know almost nothing. In that I'm not unique. Whatever research worthy of the name is being done on it has been going on behind locked doors for some time. Significant data are not released."

Telzey frowned slightly. "How do you know?"

"As soon as I learned of your curious adventures on Jontarou, I began a private investigation.

A fact-finding agency is at present assembling all available information on psionics, sorting and classifying it. Because of the general aroma of secrecy in that area, they haven't been told for whom they're working. The results they obtain are forwarded to me through the nondirect mailing system."

Oh, very good! He couldn't have arranged things better if she'd told him just what she wanted.

"How useful the material we get in that manner will be remains to be seen," Gilas concluded. "But we have two years to consider what other approaches are indicated."

Telzey took a selection of the tapes already forwarded to the bank by the fact-finding agency back to college with her. It had begun to be apparent on the return trip from Jontarou, when she was checking through the space liner's library, that there was something distinctly enigmatic about the subject of psis in the Hub. It expressed itself in the lack of information. She discovered a good deal on the government-controlled psionic machines, but what it all added up to was that they were billion-credit gadgets with mystery-shrouded circuits, which no private organization appeared able to build as yet, though a variety of them had been in public service for years.

About human psis, there was nothing worth the trouble of digging it out.

In her rooms at Pehanron that evening, she went over the fact-finding agency's tapes. Again there was nothing really new. The reflection that all this could hardly be accidental crossed her mind a number of times.

Later in the night, Telzey had her first dream of the Psionic Cop. He came tramping after her, booming something about having received complaints about her; and for some reason it scared her silly. She woke up with her heart pounding wildly and found herself demonstrating other symptoms of anxiety. After getting a glass of water, she lay down again to think about it.

It had been a rather ridiculous dream, but she still felt shaky. She almost never had nightmares. But in Psych Two she'd learned that a dream, in particular a nightmare, always symbolized something of significance to the dreamer, and there had been instructions in various self-help methods which could be used in tracking a disturbing dream down to its source.

It took around an hour to uncover the source which had produced the dream-symbol of the Psionic Cop.

There was no real question about its nature. She'd been given a set of suggestions, cunningly interwoven with various aspects of her mental life, and anchored to emotional disturbance points. When she acted against the suggestions, the disturbances were aroused. The result had been a menacing dream.

She dug at the planted thoughts for a while, then decided to leave them alone. If the Psych texts were right, nothing in her mind that she had taken a really thorough look at was going to bother her too much again.

The question was who had been interested in giving her such instructions. Who didn't want her to experiment with psionics on her own or get too curious about it?

From there on, the details began to fall into place. . . .

The odd burst of psionic noise as she came through the Customs hall at the space terminal in Orado City—Telzey considered it with a sense of apprehensive discovery.

The Customs machine certainly wasn't supposed to be able to affect human minds. But it belonged to the same family as the psionic devices of the rehabilitation centers and mental therapy institutions, which did read, manipulate, and reshape human minds. The difference, supposedly, was simply that the Customs machine was designed to do other kinds of work.

But the authority which designed, constructed and maintained all psionic machines, the Federation's Psychology Service, was at present keeping the details of design and construction a carefully guarded secret. The reason given for this was that experimentation with the machines must be carried further before such details could be offered safely to the public. Which meant that whatever the Psychology Service happened to want built into any of its machines could be built into it. And that might include something which transmitted to the mind of psis an order to either enter the Psychology Service or stop putting their special abilities to use.

That was roughly what the suggestions they'd put into her mind amounted to.

But what was the purpose?

She couldn't know immediately—and, probably, she was not supposed to be wondering. The dream had led her to discover their trick, and that had brought her to the edge of something they wouldn't want known.

It wasn't a confortable reflection. Telzey had listened to enough political shop talk among her mother's colleagues to know that the Federation could act in very decisive, ruthless ways in a matter of sufficient importance. And here was something, some plan or policy in connection with psis and psionics, apparently important enough to remain unknown even to junior members of the Federation's Grand Council! Jessamine would have expressed a very different kind of concern if she'd had any inkling that a branch of Federation government was interested in her daughter's experience with xenotelepathy.

Telzey rubbed her neck pensively. She could keep such thoughts to herself, but she couldn't very well help having them. And if the Psychology Service looked into her mind again, they might not like at all what she'd been thinking.

So what should she do?

The whole thing was connected, of course, with their top-secret psionic machines. There was one of those—a supposedly very advanced type of mind-reader, as a matter of fact—about which she could get detailed first-hand information without going farther than the Bank of Rienne. And she might learn something from that which would fill in the picture for her.

The machine was used by Transcluster Finance, the giant central bank which regulated the activities of major financial houses on more than half the Federation's worlds, and wielded more actual power than any dozen planetary governments. In the field of financial ethics. Transcluster made and enforced its own laws. Huge sums of money were frequently at stake in disputes among its associates, and machines of presumably more than human incorruptibility and accuracy were therefore employed to help settle conflicting charges and claims.

Two members of the Bank of Rienne's legal staff who specialized in ethics hearings were pleased to learn of Telzey's scholarly interest in their subject. They explained the proceedings in which the psionic Verifier was involved at considerable length. In operation, the giant telepath could draw any information pertinent to a hearing from a human mind within minutes. A participant who wished to submit his statements to verification was left alone in a heavily shielded chamber. He sensed nothing, but his mind became for a time a part of the machine's circuits. He was then released from the chamber, and the Verifier reported what it had found to the adjudicators of the hearing. The report was accepted as absolute evidence; it could not be questioned.

Rienne's attorneys felt that the introduction of psionic verification had in fact brought about a noticeable improvement in ethical standards throughout Transcluster's vast finance web. Of course it was possible to circumvent the machines. No one was obliged to make use of them; and in most cases, they were instructed to investigate only specific details of thought and memory indicated to them to confirm a particular claim. This sometimes resulted in a hearing decision going to the side which most skillfully presented the evidence in its favor for verification, rather than to the one which happened to be in the right. A Verifier was, after all, a machine and ignored whatever was not covered by its instructions, even when the mind it was scanning contained additional information with a direct and obvious bearing on the case. This had been so invariably demonstrated in practice that no reasonable person could retain the slightest qualms on the point. To further reassure those who might otherwise hesitate to permit a mind-reading machine to come into contact with them, all records of a hearing were erased from the Verifier's memory as soon as the case was closed.

And that, Telzey thought, did in a way fill in the picture. There was no evidence that Transcluster's Verifiers operated in the way they were assumed to be operating—except that for fifteen years, through innumerable hearings, they had consistently presented the appearance of being able to operate in no other manner. But the descriptions she'd been given indicated they were vaster and presumably far more complex instruments than the Customs machine at the Orado City space terminal; and from that machine— supposedly no telepath at all—an imperceptible psionic finger had flicked out, as she passed, to plant a knot of compulsive suggestions in her mind.

So what were the Verifiers doing?

One of them was set up, not at all far away, in the heart of Hub finance, a key point of the Federation. Every moment of the day, enormously important information was coming in to it from a thousand worlds—flowing through the vicinity of the Psychology Service's mind-reading device.

Could it really be restricted to scanning specific minute sections of the minds brought into contact with it in the ethics hearings?

Telzey wondered what the two amiable attorneys would say if she told them what she thought about that.

But, of course, she didn't.

It was like having wandered off-stage, accidentally and without realizing it, and suddenly finding oneself looking at something that went on behind the scenery.

Whatever the purpose of the something was, chance observers weren't likely to be welcome.

She could tiptoe away, but so long as the Psychology Service was theoretically capable of looking inside her head at any moment to see what she had been up to, that didn't change anything. Sooner or later they'd take that look. And then they'd interfere with her again, probably in a more serious manner.

So far, there seemed to be no way of getting around the advantage they had in being able to probe minds. Of course, there were such things as mind-blocks. But even if she'd known how to go about finding somebody who would be willing to equip her with one, mind-blocks were supposed to become dangerous to one's mental health when they were retained indefinitely. And if she had one, she would have to retain it indefinitely. Mind-blocks weren't the answer she wanted.

On occasion, in the days following her conversation with the ethics hearing specialists, Telzey had a very odd feeling that the answer she wanted wasn't far away. But nothing else would happen; and the feeling faded quickly. The Psionic Cop popped up in her dreams now and then, each time with less effect than before; or more rarely, he'd come briefly into her awareness after she'd been concentrated on study for a few hours. On the whole, the Cop was a minor nuisance. It looked as if the underlying compulsion had been badly shaken up by the digging around she'd done when she discovered it, and was gradually coming apart.

But that again might simply prompt the Psychology Service to take much more effective measures the next time. . . .

That was how matters stood around the beginning of the third week after Telzey's return from Jontarou. Then, one afternoon, she met an alien who was native to a non-oxygen world humans listed by a cosmographic code symbol, and who possessed a well-developed psionic talent of his own.

She had spent several hours that day in one of Orado City's major universities to gather data for a new study assignment and, on her way out, came through a hall containing a dozen or so live habitat scenes from wildly contrasting worlds. The alien was in one of the enclosures, which was about a cubic acre in size and showed an encrusted jumble of rocks lifting about the surface of an oily yellow liquid. The creature was sprawled across the rocks like a great irregular mass of translucent green jelly, with a number of variously shaped, slowly moving crimson blotches scattered through its interior.

Strange as it appeared, she was in a hurry and wouldn't have done more than glance at it through the sealing energy field which formed the transparent front wall if she hadn't caught a momentary telepathic impulse from within the enclosure as she passed. This wasn't so unusual in itself; there was, when one gave close attention to it, frequently a diffused psionic murmuring of human or animal origin or both around, but as a rule it was unaware and vague as the sound somebody might make in breathing.

The pulse that came from the alien thing seemed quite different. It could have been almost a softly whispered question, the meaningful probe of an intelligent telepath.

Telzey checked, electrified, to peer in at it. It lay motionless, and the impulse wasn't repeated. She might have been mistaken.

She shaped a thought herself, a light, unalarming "Hello, who are you?" sort of thought, and directed it gently at the green-jelly mass on the rocks.

A slow shudder ran over the thing; and then suddenly something smashed through her with numbing force. She felt herself stagger backwards, had an instant's impression of another blow coming, and of raising her arm to ward it off. Then she was somehow seated on a bench at the far end of the hall, and a uniformed attendant was asking her concernedly how she felt. It appeared she had fainted for the first time in her life. He'd picked her up off the floor and carried her to the bench.

Telzey still felt dazed, but not nearly dazed enough to tell him the truth. At the moment, she wasn't sure just what had happened back there, but it definitely was something to keep to herself. She told him the first thing to come to her mind, which was that she had skipped lunch and suddenly began to feel dizzy. That was all she remembered.

He looked somewhat relieved. "There's a cafeteria upstairs."

Telzey smiled, nodded. "I'll eat something and then I'll be all right!" She stood up.

The attendant didn't let her get away so easily. He accompanied her to the cafeteria, guiding her along by an elbow as if she were an infirm old lady. After he'd settled her at a table, he asked what she would like, and brought it to her. Then he sat down across from her.

"You do seem all right again!" he remarked at last. His anxious look wasn't quite gone. "The reason this has sort of spooked me, miss," he went on, "is something that happened around half a year ago."

"Oh? What was that?" Telzey asked carefully, sipping at the foamy chocolate-colored drink he had got for her. She wasn't at all hungry, but he obviously intended to hang around until she downed it.

There had been this other visitor, the attendant said, a well-dressed gentleman standing almost exactly where Telzey had been standing. The attendant happened to be glancing towards him when the gentleman suddenly began to stagger around, making moaning and screeching sounds, and dropped to the floor. "Only that time," the attendant said, "he was dead before we got there. And, ugh, his face . . . well, excuse me! I don't want to spoil your appetite. But it was a bad affair all around."

Telzey kept her eyes on her drink. "Did they find out what was wrong with him?"

"Something to do with his heart, they told me." The attendant looked at her doubtfully. "Well, I suppose it must have been his heart. It's just that those are very peculiar creatures they keep in that hall. It can make you nervous working around them."

"What kind of creatures are they?" Telzey asked.

He shook his head, said they didn't have names. Federation expeditions brought them back from one place and another, and they were maintained here, each in its made-to-order environment, so the scientists from the university could study them. In his opinion, they were such unnatural beasts that the public should be barred from the hall; but he didn't make the rules. Of course, there was actually no way they could hurt anybody from inside the habitat tanks, not through those force fields. But it had unnerved him today to see another visitor topple over before that one particular tank. . . .

He returned to his duties finally, and Telzey pushed her empty glass aside and considered the situation.

By now, every detail of what happened there had returned to her memory. The green-jelly creature definitely did hurt people through the energy screens around its enclosure . . . if the people happened to be telepaths. In them it found mental channels through which it could send savage surges of psi force. So the unfortunate earlier visitor had been a psi, who responded as unsuspectingly as she did to the alien's probing whisper, and then met quick death.

She'd fallen into the same trap, but escaped. In the first instant of stunned confusion, already losing consciousness, she'd had a picture of herself raising her arm to block the creature's blows. She hadn't done it, of course; the blows weren't physical ones, and couldn't be blocked in that manner. But in the same reflexive, immediate manner, she'd done something else, not even knowing what she did, but doing it simply because it was the only possible defensive move she could have made at that instant, and in that particular situation.

Now she knew what the move had been. Something that seemed as fragile as a soap bubble was stretched about her mind. But it wasn't fragile. It was a curtain of psi energy she'd brought into instant existence to check the creature's psi attacks as her senses blacked out.

It was still there, unchanged, maintaining itself with no further effort on her part. She could tell that it would, in fact, take a deliberate effort to destructure it again—and she had no intention of doing that until she was a good, long distance away from the hostile mind in the habitat tank downstairs.

Although it needn't be, Telzey thought, a particularly hostile creature. Perhaps it had simply acted as it would have done on its own world where other telepathic creatures might be a natural prey, to be tricked into revealing themselves as they came near, and then struck down.

In a public park, ten minutes later, she sat down in a quiet place where she could make an undisturbed investigation of her psi bubble and its properties. After an hour or so, she decided she had learned enough about it for the moment, and went back to the hall of the live habitat scenes. There was a different attendant on duty now, and half-a-dozen other people were peering in at the occupant of one of the other tanks.

Telzey settled down on a bench opposite the enclosure of the green-jelly alien. He lay unmoving on his rocks and gave no indication of being aware of her return. She opened a section of the bubble, and sent him a sharp "You, there!" thought. A definitely unfriendly thought.

At once, he slammed back at her with a violence which seemed to shake the hall all around her. But the bubble was closed again, and there were no other effects. The attendant and the people farther down the hall obviously hadn't sensed anything. This was a matter strictly between psis.

Telzey let a minute or so pass before she gave the creature another prodding thought. This time, he was slower to react, and when he did, it was with rather less enthusiasm. He mightn't have liked the experience of having his thrusts bounced back by the bubble.

He had killed a human psi and tried to kill her, but she felt no real animosity towards him. He was simply too different for that. She could, however, develop a hate-thought if she worked at it, and she did. Then she opened the bubble and shot it at him.

The outworld thing shuddered. He struck back savagely and futilely. She lashed him with hate again, and he shuddered again.

Minutes later, he suddenly went squirming and flowing down the rocks and into the oily yellow liquid that washed around them. He was attempting panicky flight, and there was nowhere to go. Telzey stood up carefully and went over to the enclosure, where she could see him bunched up against the far side beneath the surface. He gave the impression of being very anxious to avoid further trouble with her. She opened the bubble wider than before, though still with some caution, picked out his telepathic channels and followed them into his mind. There was no resistance, but she flinched a little. The impression she had—translated very roughly into human terms—was of terrified, helpless sobbing. The creature was waiting to be killed.

She studied the strange mind a few minutes longer, then drew away from it, and left the habitat hall. It wouldn't be necessary to do anything else about the green-jelly alien. He wasn't very intelligent, but he had an excellent memory.

And never, never, never, would he attempt to attack one of the terrible human psis again.

Telzey had a curious feeling about the bubble. It was something with which she had seemed immediately more than half familiar. Letting it flick into being and out again soon was as automatic as opening and closing her eyes. And in tracing out the delicate manipulations by which its wispiest sections could be controlled and shifted, she had the impression of merely needing to refresh her memory about details already known. . . . This, of course, was the way to go about that! That was how it worked. . . .

There had been that other tantalizing feeling recently. Of being very close to an answer to her problems with the Psychology Service, but not quite able to see it. Perhaps the bubble had begun to form in response to her need for an answer and the awareness of it would have come to her gradually if the alien's attack hadn't brought it out to be put to instant emergency use. It was a fluid pattern, drawing the psi energy that sustained it from unknown sources, as if there were an invisible ocean of psi nearby to which she had put out a tap. She had heard of soft-bodied, vulnerable creatures which survived by fitting themselves into the discarded hard shells of other creatures and trudging about in them. The bubble was a little like that, though the other way around—something she had shaped to fit her; not a part of herself, but a marvelously delicate and adjustable apparatus which should have many uses beyond turning into a solid suit of psi armor in emergencies.

At the moment, for example, it might be used to prepare a deceptive image of herself to offer to future Psychology Service investigators. . . .

That took several days. Then, so far as Telzey could tell, any significant thinking she did about psionics, or the Psychology Service and its machines, would produce only the blurriest of faint traces under a telepathic probe. The same for her memories on the subject, back to the night when she'd been scared out of sleep by her first dream of the Psionic Cop. And the explanation was that the Cop had scared her so that she'd lost her interest in the practice of telepathy then and there.

Since their suggestion had been to do just that, they might buy it. On the other hand, if they took a really careful look into her mind, the thought-camouflage might not fool them long, or even for an instant. But they'd have to start searching around then to find out what really had been going on; and if they touched any part of the bubble block, she should know it. She had made other preparations for that.

In a rented deposit vault of the nondirect mailing system in Orado City there was a stack of addressed and arrival-dated microtapes, all with an identical content; and on Telzey's wrist-talker were two new tiny control buttons keyed to the vault. Five minutes after she pressed down the first button, the tapes would be launched into the automatic mazes of the nondirect system, where nothing could intercept or identify them until they reached their individual destinations. She could stop the process by depressing the second button before the five minutes were up, but in no other manner. The tapes contained the thinking she'd done about the psionic machines. It might be only approximately correct, but it still was a kind of thinking the Psychology Service would not want to see broadcast at random to the news media of the Hub.

It wasn't a wholly satisfactory solution for a

number of reasons, including the one that she couldn't know just what she might start by pushing the button. But it would have to do until she thought of something better. If there were indications of trouble, simply revealing that she could push it should make everybody quite careful for the moment. And after completing her preparations, she hadn't actually been expecting trouble, at least not for some while. She was behaving in a very innocuous manner, mainly busy with her legitimate studies; and that checked with the picture presented by the thought-camouflage. She'd talked about telepathy only to Gilas and Gonwil, telling Gonwil just enough to make sure she wouldn't mention the esoteric tapes Telzey occasionally immersed herself in to somebody else.

Now, of course, that might change to some extent. As Gilas had implied, they couldn't risk holding back information from the detectives he was employing because what they withheld might turn out to have been exactly the information the detectives had needed. If they were as discreet as Gilas thought, it probably wouldn't matter much.

Telzey twisted her mouth doubtfully, staring at the thin, smoky lines of air traffic converging far ahead of Orado City. . . .

Probably, it wouldn't!

IX

SEVERAL HOURS after Telzey's departure, Pehanron College's buildings and grounds, spreading up the sun-soaked hills above the residential town of Beale, were still unusually quiet.

Almost half the student body was struggling with mid-summer examinations, and a good proportion of those who had finished had obtained permission to get off to an early start for the holidays. The carports extending along the backs of the student courts showed a correspondingly large number of vacancies, though enough gleaming vehicles remained to have supplied the exhibits for the average aircar show, a fair percentage running up into the price ranges of small interstellar freighters. Pehanron sometimes was accused of opening its lists only to the sons and daughters of millionaires; and while this wasn't strictly true, the college did scout assiduously for such of them as might be expected to maintain the pace of its rugged curriculum. Pehanron liked to consider itself a select hatchery from which sprang a continuous line of leaders in many fields of achievement, and as a matter of fact, it did turn out more than its share of imposing names.

There was no one in sight in Court Ninety-two when Senior Counselor Eulate turned into it, arriving from the direction of the managerial offices. Miss Eulate was a plump, brisk little woman whose normal expression when she felt unobserved was a vaguely worried frown. The frown was somewhat pronounced at the moment.

At the gate of the duplex bungalow marked 18-19, the counselor came to an abrupt stop. In the center of the short garden path, head and pointed wolf ears turned in her direction, lay a giant white dog of the type known as Askanam arena hounds—a breed regarded, so Miss Eulate had been told, as the ultimate in reckless canine ferocity and destructiveness when aroused.

The appearance of Chomir—a yellow-eyed, extravagantly muscled hundred-and-fifty-pounder—always brought this information only too vividly back to Miss Eulate's mind. Not wishing to arouse the silently staring monster now, she continued to hesitate at the gate. Then, hearing the intermittent purr of a tapewriter from beyond the open door at the end of the path, she called out in a carefully moderate tone. "Gonwil?"

The tapewriter stopped. Gonwil's voice replied, "Yes . . . is that you, Miss Eulate?"

"It is. Please keep an eye on Chomir while I come in."

"Oh, for goodness sake!" Gonwil appeared laughing in the door. She was eighteen; a good-looking, limber-bodied, sunny-tempered blonde. "Now you know Chomir won't hurt you! He *likes* you!"

Miss Eulate's reply was a skeptical silence. But she proceeded up the path now, giving the giant hound a wary four feet of clearance as she went by. To her relief Chomir didn't move until she was past; then he merely placed his massive head back on his forelegs and half closed his eyes. Airily ignoring Gonwil's amused smile, Miss Eulate indicated the closed entrance door on the other side of the duplex as she came up. "Telzey isn't still asleep?"

"No, she left early. Did you want to see her?" Miss Eulate shook her head.

"This concerns you," she said. "It would be better if we went inside."

In Gonwil's study, she brought a note pad and a small depth photo from her pocket. She held out the pad. "Do these names mean anything to you?"

Gonwil took the pad curiously. After a moment, she shook her head.

"No. Should they?"

Looking as stern as her chubby features permitted, Miss Eulate handed her the photo. "Then do you know these two people?"

Gonwil studied the two figures briefly, said, "To the best of my knowledge, I've never seen either of them, Miss Eulate. What is this about?"

"The Tayun consulate in Orado City had the picture transmitted to us a short while ago," Miss Eulate said. "The two persons in it—giving the names I showed you—called the consulate earlier in the morning and inquired about you."

"What did they want?"

"They said they had learned you were in Orado and would like to know where you could be found. They implied they were personal friends of yours from Tayun."

The girl shook her head. "They may be from Tayun, but we aren't even casually acquainted. I . . ."

"The consulate," Miss Eulate said grimly, "suspected as much! They secretly recorded the screen images of the callers, who were then re- quested to come to the consulate to be satisfactor- ily identified while your wishes in the matter were determined. The callers agreed but have failed to show up. The consulate feels this may indicate criminal intentions. I understand you have been placed on record there as being in- volved in a private war on Tayun, and . . ."

"Oh, no!" Gonwil wrinkled her nose in sudden dismay. "Not that nonsense again! Not just now!"

"Please don't feel alarmed!" Miss Eulate told her, not without a trace of guilty relish. The counselor took a strong vicarious interest in the personal affairs of her young charges, and to find one of them touched by the dangerous glamor of a private war was undeniably exciting. "Nobody can harm you here," she went on. "Pehanron maintains a very dependable security system to safeguard its students."

"I'm sure it does," Gonwil said. "But frankly, Miss Eulate, I don't need to be safeguarded and I'm not at all alarmed."

"You aren't?" Miss Eulate asked, surprised.

"No. Whatever reason these people had for pretending to be friends of mine . . . I can think of several perfectly harmless ones . . . they aren't vendettists."

"Vendettists?"

Gonwil smiled. "Commercial vendetta. An old

custom on Tayun—a special kind of private war. A couple of generations ago it was considered good form to kill off your business competitors if you could. It isn't being done so much any more, but the practice hasn't entirely died out."

Miss Eulate's eyebrows rose. "But then . . ."

"Well, the point is," Gonwil said, "that I'm not involved in any vendetta or private war! And I never have been, except in Cousin Malrue's imagination."

"I don't understand," the counselor said. "Cousin Malrue . . . you're referring to Mrs. Parlin?"

"Yes. She isn't exactly a cousin but she's the closest relative I have. In fact, the only one. And I'm very fond of her. I practically grew up in the Parlin family . . . and of course they've more or less expected that Junior and I would eventually get married."

Miss Eulate nodded. "Rodel Parlin the Twelfth. Yes, I know." She had met the young man several times on his visits to the college to see Gonwil and gained an excellent impression of him. It looked like an eminently suitable match, one of which Pehanron would certainly have approved; but regrettably Gonwil had not returned Rodel Parlin the Twelfth's very evident affection in kind.

"Now, Cousin Malrue," Gonwil went on, "has always been afraid that one or the other of my father's old business enemies on Tayun was going to try to have me killed before I came of age. My parents and my uncle—my father's brother—founded Lodis Associates and made a pretty big splash in Tayun's financial world right

from the start. Malrue and her husband joined
the concern before I was born, and then, when I
was about a year and a half old, my parents and
my uncle were killed in two separate accidents.
Cousin Malrue was convinced it was vendetta
action. . . ."

"Mightn't it have been?" Miss Eulate asked.

Gonwil shrugged. "She had some reason for
suspecting it at the time. My parents and uncle
apparently had been rather ruthless in the
methods they used to build up Lodis Associates,
and no doubt they had plenty of enemies. The
authorities who investigated the matter said very
definitely that the deaths had been accidental,
but Malrue didn't accept that.

"Then, after the directors of a Tayun bank had
been appointed my guardians, some crank sent
them a message. It said my parents had died as a
result of the evil they'd done, and that their
daughter would never live to handle the money
they had robbed from better people than themselves. You can imagine what effect that had on
Cousin Malrue!"

"Yes, I believe I can."

"And that," Gonwil said, "is really the whole
story. Since then, every time it's looked as if I
might have come close to being in an accident or
getting harmed in some way, Cousin Malrue has
taken it for granted that vendettists were behind
it. The thing has simply preyed on her mind!"

Miss Eulate looked doubtful, asked, "Isn't it
possible that you are taking the matter too lightly, Gonwil? As you may remember, I met Mrs.
Parlin on one occasion here. We had quite an
extensive conversation, and she impressed me as

being a very intelligent and levelheaded person."

"Oh, she is," Gonwil said. "Don't misunderstand me. Cousin Malrue is in fact the most intelligent woman I've ever known. She's been running Lodis Associates almost singlehandedly for the past fifteen years, and the firm's done very well in that time.

"No, it's just that one subject on which she isn't reasonable. Nobody can argue her out of the idea that vendettists are lurking for me. It's very unfortunate that those mysterious strangers, whoever they were, should have showed up just now. By Tayun's laws I'll become a responsible adult on the day I'm nineteen, and that's only three months away."

Miss Eulate considered, nodded. "I see! You will then be able to handle the money left to you by your parents. So if the vendettists want to make good on their threat, they would have to, uh, eliminate you before that day!"

"Uh-huh," Gonwil said. "Actually, of course, most of the money stays in Lodis Associates, but from then on I'll have a direct voice in the concern's affairs. The Parlin family and I own about seventy per cent of the stock between us. I suppose those nonexistent vendettists would consider that the same thing as handling my parents' money."

Miss Eulate was silent a moment. "If the people who called the consulate were not the vendettists," she said, "why should they have behaved in such a suspicious manner?"

Gonwil laughed ruefully.

"Miss Eulate, I do believe you could become

almost as bad as Cousin Malrue about this! Why, they might have had any number of reasons for acting as they did. If they were from Tayun, they could know I'd soon be of age and they might have some business they'd like me to put money in. Or perhaps they just didn't express themselves clearly enough, and they're actually friends of some friends of mine who asked them to look me up on Orado. Or they could be from a Tayun news agency, looking for a story on the last member of the Lodis family. You see?"

"Well, there are such possibilities, of course," the counselor conceded. "However, I fail to understand then why you appear to be concerned about Mrs. Parlin's reactions. If nothing comes of the matter, isn't it quite unlikely that she'll ever learn that somebody has inquired about you?"

"Ordinarily, it would be," Gonwil said glumly. "But she and Rodel the Eleventh are due to arrive on Orado at almost any moment. I'd been expecting them the day after tomorrow, but Junior called an hour ago to say the schedule had changed, and they'd be here today. Malrue is bound to find out what happened, and, to put it mildly, she's going to be extremely upset!"

"Yes, no doubt." Miss Eulate hesitated, went on. "I dislike to tell you this, but it's been decided that until a satisfactory explanation for the appearance of the two strangers at the consulate has been obtained, certain steps will have to be taken to insure your personal safety. You understand that the college has a contractual obligation to your guardians to see that no harm comes to you while you are a student."

Gonwil looked at her, asked, "Meaning I'm restricted to the campus?"

"I'm afraid we'll have to go a little farther than that. We are assigning guards to see to it that no unauthorized persons enter bungalow 18-19, and I must instruct you not to leave it for the next day or two."

"Oh, dear! And all because . . ." Gonwil shook her blonde head. "Cousin Malrue will have kittens when she hears that!"

The counselor looked surprised.

"But why should Mrs. Parlin have, uh, kittens?" she inquired. "Surely she will see that the college is acting only to keep you out of possible danger!"

"She simply won't believe I'm not in danger here, Miss Eulate! When my guardians enrolled me at Pehanron, she didn't at all like the idea of my coming to Orado by myself. That's why the college has had to put up with that monster Chomir for the past two years! My guardians thought it would calm Malrue down if I kept one of the famous Askanam arena hounds around as a bodyguard. They sent all the way there to get one of the best."

Miss Eulate nodded. "I see. I . . ." Her voice died in her throat.

Moving with ghostly quiet, Chomir had appeared suddenly in the doorway to the garden. He stood there, yellow eyes fixed on them.

"He heard me use his name and came to see if I'd called him," Gonwil said apologetically. "I'll send him back out till we're finished."

"No," the counselor said with some firmness,

"tell him to come in. I shouldn't allow him to frighten me, and I know it. Now is as good a time as any to overcome that weakness!"

Gonwil looked pleased. "Come on in, boy!"

The Askanam came forward, moving lightly and easily in spite of his size. In the patch of sunlight from the door, an ivory brindle pattern was faintly visible in the short white hair of his hide, the massive cables of surface muscle shifting and sliding beneath it. Miss Eulate, for all her brave words just now, felt her mouth go parched. Ordinarily she liked dogs, and Chomir was a magnificent dog. But there were those stories about his breed—merciless killers developed by painstaking geneticists to perform in the bloody arenas of Askanam and to provide the ruling nobility of that colorful and tempestuous world with the most incorruptible and savage of guards. . . .

"I imagine," the counselor observed uncomfortably, "that Chomir would, in fact, be an excellent protector for you if it became necessary."

"No doubt about that," Gonwil agreed. "And I very much hope it never becomes necessary. It would be a fearful mess! Have I told you what happened when they were going to teach him how to defend me?"

"No, you haven't," Miss Eulate acknowledged, wishing she hadn't brought up the subject.

"It was just before I left for Orado. My guardians had hired an Askanam dog trainer. Chomir wasn't much more than a pup then, but when they're training arena dogs on Askanam, they don't use human beings to simulate an attacker.

They use special robots which look and move and smell like human beings.

"I found out why! They turned two of those poor machines loose on me, and Chomir shook both of them to pieces before I could shout, 'Stop!' The trainer told me that when he's really clamping his jaws down on something, he slams on close to two thousand pounds of pressure."

"Good heavens!" Miss Eulate said faintly.

"Anyway," Gonwil went on, unaware of the effect she was creating, "everyone decided right then that one thing Chomir didn't need was attack training!" She prodded the dog's hard flank affectionately with a shoe tip. "Of course, he does have a terrific pedigree to account for it. His sire was a famous arena dog who killed thirty-two men and all kinds of fighting animals. He must have been a pretty horrible beast! And on his dam's side . . ."

She broke off, having finally caught Miss Eulate's expression, went on after a moment, "I don't really mind so much being confined to quarters. But I'm hoping the mystery at the consulate will be solved before the Parlins arrive. There's no possible way I could avoid seeing Malrue, and . . ."

She checked herself for the second time, added in a different tone, "That's Junior calling again now!"

"Eh?" Miss Eulate asked. Then, following Gonwil's gaze, she became aware of a faint, silvery tinkling from the table. A tiny, jewel-bright device stood there, out of which the sound evidently came. On closer inspection, it appeared to be a beautifully inlaid power compact. Miss Eulate looked puzzledly back at the girl.

"A personalized communicator," Gonwil explained wryly. "A gift from Junior which came in the mail this morning. He has the twin to it, and the only use for the set is that Junior and I can talk together wherever either of us happens to be on Orado." She gave Miss Eulate a small smile, added, "Junior is very difficult to discourage!"

The miniature communicator stopped its tinkling for a few seconds, then began again. Gonwil still made no move towards it. Miss Eulate asked, "Aren't you going to answer him?"

"No. If I don't switch it on, he'll think I'm not around."

Miss Eulate sighed and arose.

"Well," she said, "I should get back to the office. We'll trust this has been as you feel, a false alarm. But until we're quite certain of it, we must take whatever precautions seem indicated."

Gonwil grimaced resignedly.

The counselor went on, "And since the Bank of Rienne is acting as your guardians on Orado, I'm also obliged to see to it that they are informed of the occurrence."

At that, Gonwil's face suddenly brightened.

"Miss Eulate," she said, "when you make that call . . . and please make it at once . . . would you have it put through directly to Mr. Amberdon?"

"Why, yes, I can do that. But why specifically Mr. Amberdon?"

"He may be able to do something. Besides, Telzey's gone to see him. She should be with him just about this time—and she can usually think of a way out of anything."

"I'm quite aware of it," Miss Eulate said, rather shortly. Privately she regarded Telzey, in spite of her unquestioned scholastic brilliance, as something of a college problem. She added, "Well, I'll see what can be done."

X

THERE HAD BEEN enough general activity during
the past two hours to leave Telzey unaware, except for a fleeting moment now and then, that
she had begun to feel some physical effects of
having passed up the night's sleep.

She couldn't, she thought, have complained
that her warning wasn't taken seriously! Of
course, the fact that Gonwil was a temporary
ward of the bank would have required that it be
given attention, even without the backing of the
personal interest of Rienne's executive officer
and his daughter.

A query regarding the internal structure of the
Tayun concern of Lodis Associates had gone to
Transcluster Finance Central almost immediately after her call to Gilas, and she had
barely arrived at the bank when a reply came
back.

Transcluster's records confirmed in every particular what she had gathered in casual talk with
Gonwil from time to time and failed to give its
proper significance. Lodis Associates basically
had been set up in a manner which tended to
leave control of the concern with the founding
associates and their heirs. Shares could be sold
only after being offered to all other associates at

the original value. Since the original value had been approximately a twentieth of the present one, current sales to outsiders were in effect blocked. If a deceased associate left no natural heirs, his stock was distributed among the surviving associates in proportion to their holdings.

Which meant that Gonwil's death would in fact place the Parlin family in control of the concern . . .

And that seemed enough to convince both Gilas and Wellan Dasinger, the chief of the Kyth Detective Agency, who had arrived before Telzey, that the danger was real. It puzzled her because it hardly looked like conclusive proof of anything, but she decided they were aware of possibilities in situations of that kind which she couldn't know about. Within an hour, the Bank of Rienne and the Kyth Agency had initiated cluster-spanning activities on behalf of the bank's temporary ward which would have stunned Gonwil if she'd been told about them.

So much action should have been reassuring. But her father and Dasinger still looked worried; and presently Gilas appeared to realize again that she was around, and explained. It was a delicate situation. As Gonwil's appointed local guardian, the bank could act with a certain amount of authority; but that advantage was based on a technicality which could be shattered in an instant by her guardians on Tayun. "And they're aware, of course—at least in a general way—of Mrs. Parlin's plans."

Telzey gave him a startled look. "Why should . . ."

"Since Gonwil was a minor," Gilas said. "her guardians could have taken legal steps to nullify the condition that her death would benefit the other members of Lodis Associates. And considering that business practices on Tayun remain close to the level of tribal warfare, they *would* have done it—automatically on assuming guardianship—unless it was to their own benefit to be a little negligent about the matter."

"Her own guardians would help Malrue kill Gonwil?" Telzey said incredulously.

"Probably not directly. And of course if Gonwil had decided to marry the son, no one would have had any reason to kill her. But as it stands, we must expect that her guardians will try to hamper any obvious efforts now to protect her against Malrue Parlin. So we have to be very careful not to reveal our suspicions at present. Until we can get Gonwil's formal request to represent her in the matter, we'll be on very shaky legal ground if we're challenged from Tayun. And from what I know of Gonwil, it's going to be difficult for her to accept that she might be in danger from Mrs. Parlin."

Telzey nodded. "We'll almost have to prove it first."

Dasinger put in, "Supposing—this is a theoretical question—but supposing this turned into a situation where Miss Lodis saw that in order to stay alive herself it might be necessary to have Mrs. Parlin killed. Knowing her as you do, do you think she could be brought to agree to the action?"

Telzey stared at the detective, realized with

some shock that he had been speaking seriously, that it wasn't a theoretical question at all.

She said carefully, "I can't imagine her agreeing to any such thing, Mr. Dasinger! She just isn't a—a violent person. I don't think she's ever intentionally hurt anybody."

"And of course," the detective said, "the Parlin family, having known her since infancy, is quite aware of that."

"Yes . . . I suppose so." It was another disturbing line of thought. Gilas said quickly, smiling, "Well, we don't intend to let it come to that. In a general way though, Telzey, Gonwil's attitudes are likely to be a handicap here. We'll see how well we can work around them for now."

She didn't answer. There was, of course—as Gilas knew—a way to change Gonwil's attitudes. But it didn't seem necessary to mention that immediately.

Wellan Dasinger, who might be Gilas's junior by seven or eight years, had an easy tone and manner and didn't seem too athletically built. But somehow one gradually got the impression that he was the sort of man who would start off each day with forty push-ups and a cold needle shower as a matter of course. Telzey didn't know what his reaction had been when Gilas told him she'd been getting information from the mind of a dog, but he discussed it with her as if it were perfectly normal procedure. Kyth operatives had been dispatched to Beale to look around for the mysterious stranger of Chomir's memories; and Dasinger, unhurriedly and thoughtfully, went over every detail she had obtained, then questioned her at length about Gonwil's relationship to the Parlins, the vendetta stories, the maneuvering to get Gonwil married to Junior.

There seemed to be no question of Dasinger's competence. And it was clear he didn't like the situation.

Information began flowing back from Tayun over interstellar transmitters from various contacts of the bank and Dasinger's agency. One item seemed to provide all the evidence needed to indicate that caution was advisable in dealing with the Parlin family. During the past two decades, the number of shareholders in Lodis Associates had diminished by almost fifty per cent. The last three to go had dropped out simultaneously after transferring their holdings to Malrue Parlin, following a disagreement with her on a matter of company policy. Some of the others had taken the same route, but rather more had died in one way or another. There had never been any investigation of the deaths. The remaining associates appeared to be uniformly staunch supporters of Mrs. Parlin's policies.

Dasinger didn't like that either.

"Leaving out crude measures like counterviolence," he told Telzey, "there probably are going to be just two methods to make sure your friend gets a chance to enjoy a normal life span. One of them is to route Mrs. Parlin into Rehabilitation. If she's tamed down, the rest of the clique shouldn't be very dangerous. She's obviously the organizer."

Telzey asked uncertainly, "What's the other method?"

"Have Miss Lodis hand over her stock to Mrs. Parlin for whatever she's willing to pay. I doubt it would be safe to argue too strongly about the price."

Telzey was silent a moment. "Supposing," she said finally, "that Gonwil did agree to . . . well, counterviolence. That would be a private war—"

"Yes, we'd have to register to make it legitimate."

"You—your agency—handles private wars?"

"Occasionally we'll handle one," Dasinger said. "It depends on the client and the circumstances. I'd say this is such an occasion."

She looked at him. "Isn't that pretty risky work?"

The detective pursed his lips judiciously.

"No, not too risky. It would be expensive and messy. Mrs. Parlin appears to be an old hand at this, but we'd restrict the main action to Orado. If she imported her own talent, they'd be at a severe disadvantage here. And the better local boys wouldn't want any part of it after we got word around that the Kyth Agency was representing the other side. We should have the thing settled, without placing Miss Lodis in jeopardy, in about six months, even if we had to finish up on Tayun. But it appears Miss Lodis has a prejudice against such methods."

"Yes, she does," Telzey said. After a moment, she added, "So do I."

"I don't know about your friend, Miss Amberdon," Dasinger said pleasantly, "but I expect you'll grow out of it. At the moment though, it seems our line should be to try to manipulate Mrs. Parlin into Rehabilitation. We should know inside an hour about how good a chance we'll have to do it. I'm waiting for a call."

The call came in ten minutes later. It was from the Kyth Agency.

There appeared to be much Pehanron's law courses hadn't mentioned about the practical aspects of mind-blocks.

The Tayun connection's report to the agency was that the Parlin family had been for years on the official list of those who were provided with mind-blocks for general commercial reasons. These, Dasinger explained, were expensive, high-precision jobs which ordinarily did not restrict their possessor in any noticeable way. But when specific levels of stress or fatigue were developed, the block automatically cut in to prevent the divulging of information from the areas it was set to cover.

"You see how it works," Dasinger said. "You have the block installed, have its presence officially confirmed, and have the fact published. Thereafter, nobody who's bothered to check the list will attempt to extort the information from you, because they know you can't give it. The Rehabilitation machines supposedly can take down any block, but they might need a year. Otherwise, nothing I've ever heard of can get much through a solidly installed block—continuous questioning, drugs, mind-probes, threats, torture, enforced sleeplessness, hypnotics. All that can be accomplished is to kill the blocked person eventually, and if that's your goal there're easier ways of going about it."

Apparently, too, the fancier type of block did not bring on the mental deterioration she'd heard about. Malrue Parlin's faculties obviously hadn't been impaired.

"A commercial block of that nature," Gilas said slowly, "presumably would cover plans to murder a business associate for profit in any case." He looked as if he'd bitten into something sour. "When it comes to the Parlins, we can be sure it would cover them. There've been a number of occasions when Mrs. Parlin must have banked on that for protection if an investigation should catch up with her."

"Getting rid of unwanted fellow associates was a business matter, so the block would automatically cover any action to that end," Dasinger agreed.

Gilas rubbed his chin, took out a cigarette, lit it. He scowled absently at Telzey.

"Then circumstantial evidence isn't going to get us anywhere against the lady," he said. "Either in Federation court or in a Transcluster hearing. It's too bad, because in a few hours this morning we've accumulated almost enough evidence to force the Parlins to clear themselves through a subjective probe. After we've sorted it over, we might find we have enough. But a subjective probe would simply confirm that they're equipped with blocks. Tampering with a recognized block is legally equivalent to manslaughter. That would end our case." He looked at the detective. "So what do you suggest?"

"A trap," Dasinger said. "Now, before they find out they're suspected. Later on they wouldn't be likely to fall for it."

"And how do we go about it?"

"My boys are trying to locate Junior. We're not

sure he's in Orado City; at any rate, he hasn't checked in at his hotel. But they should have his rooms tapped for view and sound by now, and when they find him, they'll keep watch on him around the clock.

"Two days from now, when his parents arrive, we should be able to have them under observation before they leave the spaceport. There's no reason to think they'll be taking extraordinary precautions at that time, so we should very shortly pick up enough of the conversation between them and Junior to know what their plans are.

"If the plans include the immediate murder of Miss Lodis, we'll go along with it. And with a little luck, we'll catch either the Parlins themselves or somebody who can be proved to be their agent in the actual attempt to commit murder. If they're to wind up in Rehabilitation, we shouldn't try to settle for anything less definite."

He turned to Telzey. "Naturally, Miss Lodis won't be the bait for our trap. We'll have a decoy, someone who can impersonate her to the extent required. But meanwhile we may have a difficult problem in keeping her out of the way without tipping our hand—unless, of course, something can be done immediately to weaken her trust in Mrs. Parlin."

He'd said it very casually. But he might know more about what a psi could accomplish in that direction than he'd indicated. And she could do it. It would take some time; she had found making the initial contact with the mind of a nonpsi human an involved and rather difficult process—something very different from getting into an exchange with other telepaths, and more involved by a good bit than the same proceeding had been with Chomir. But then Gonwil wouldn't realize she was being influenced in any way while her lifelong feelings about Cousin Malrue began to change. . . .

Telzey said, "I arranged with Gonwil that we'd start out on a holiday trip together after I get back to the college today. We'll take Chomir along. If we can find some place where there isn't too much disturbance—"

Dasinger smiled, nodded. "We'll take care of that."

"Then," Telzey said. "I think I could talk Gonwil into co-operating with us—before Mr. and Mrs. Parlin get here."

"That would be very helpful! And now the dog . . . you mentioned that you should be able to find out exactly why the dog considers that unidentified stranger to be an enemy."

"Yes," Telzey said. Unless she was mistaken, Dasinger had a very fair picture of what she intended to do about Gonwil; and that explained, of course, why he'd accepted her account of Chomir's adventures without question. He did know something about psis. "I think I could get that from him in another couple of hours," she said. "We'd come pretty close to it before I had to stop this morning."

She left the office area a few minutes later to pick up the Cloudsplitter and start back to Pehanron. She had a plan of her own, but it would be best to wait until they had Gonwil under cover before mentioning it. Gilas mightn't like it; but she'd talk to Dasinger first to find out if it might be feasible to plant her somewhere in the immediate vicinity of the Parlins after they arrived. Gonwil would be co-operating by that time; and while she didn't know whether she could get into a mind that was guarded by a block, it would be worth trying it if she could remain unobserved around Malrue long enough to carry out the preliminary work.

Because if she could do it, they'd do better than find out what the murder plans were. Without knowing why, Malrue would quietly give up her evil intentions towards Gonwil within a few hours, and remain incapable of developing them again or permitting her husband and son to carry on. And that would settle the whole matter in the simplest possible way.

She was approaching the exits to the upper level parking strip where she had left the Cloudsplitter when somebody addressed her.

"Miss Amberdon! One moment, please!"

It was one of the bank guards. Telzey stopped. "Yes?"

"Mr. Amberdon's secretary notified us just now to watch for you here," the guard explained. "There's an open line to her office in this com-booth. She said to tell you a very important matter had come up, and you should hear about it before leaving the building."

Telzey slipped into the booth, frowning. Gilas could have reached her through her wrist-talker while she was in the bank . . . perhaps he didn't want to chance being overheard by some stray beam-tapper. The door closed automatically behind her as she touched the ComWeb's button, and Ravia, Gilas's blue-haired, highly glamorous and highly efficient secretary, appeared in the screen.

"I thought they might still catch you," she said, smiling. "Your father would like to speak to you on a shielded line, Telzey. You're on one now, and I'll connect you with him."

Her image faded. Gilas came on, said briskly, "There you are! There's been a change of schedule. Take your car down to the general parking area. You'll find two of Dasinger's men waiting for you with a carrier. They'll load on your car and take you back to Pehanron with them. We'll brief you on the way."

"What's happened?" she asked, startled.

"We've had a very unpleasant surprise. You'd barely left when two items of information came in. The first was that Mr. and Mrs. Parlin were found listed among the passengers of a ship which berthed at the space terminal something over an hour ago. We're having the Orado City hotels checked, but we don't know where the pair is at present. And Junior hasn't been found yet."

Telzey swallowed.

"Then," Gilas went on, "I had a call from Pehanron College. I'll give you the details on that a little later. What it seems to amount to is that the Parlins have succeeded in creating an atmosphere of alarm and confusion regarding Gonwil's safety, which should serve to keep suspicions turned well away from them if something actually happens to her. One result is that special measures will be needed now to get Gonwil away from Pehanron without dangerous delay. You probably could handle that part of it better than any outsider. Do you want to try it?"

"Yes, of course," she said.

Telzey discovered the hand that rested on the screen button was trembling a little.

"All right," Gilas gave her a brief smile. "I'll tell you the rest of it after you're in the carrier."

The screen went blank.

"And all I've been trying to do all morning," Gonwil exclaimed, somewhere between laughter and dismay, "was to settle down quietly without interruptions to get those grisly Finance Eleven tapes cleaned up! You'd think everybody had gone out of their minds!"

Telzey looked sympathetic. Gonwil's lunch had been delivered to her in the duplex, on Miss Eulate's instructions; and a few college guards in civilian clothes loafed around outside, trying to look as if they'd just happened to wander into the area and weren't really much interested in anything here. Gonwil filled Telzey in on the morning's events while she ate the lunch and Telzey thoughtfully sipped a mug of milk. The first thing Malrue Parlin and her husband had done after landing at Orado City's spaceport was to check in at the Tayun consulate. The first thing the consul general there, an old acquaintance, had done was to tell them about the ominous strangers who had inquired about Gonwil Lodis early in the day. And the fat was in the fire.

"Cousin Malrue went into a howling tizzy!" Gonwil reported, shuddering. "She said she'd always known it was too risky for me to be studying on Orado. So she wanted to get me away from here now, with the Parlin family, where I'd be safe. Naturally, Pehanron said, 'No!'—and am I glad! Old Eulate's bad enough about this, but Malrue . . .!''

"Think she might pop in on you here?"

Gonwil noddded. "The whole family plans to show up at Pehanron this evening. Malrue will be battling with Eulate—and I'll be in the middle! And there's no way I can stop it."

"You wouldn't be in the middle," Telzey observed, "if you weren't here."

"If I weren't . . ." Gonwil glanced sharply over at her, lowered her voice to a whisper. "How . . . when Eulate's got those people staring at my front and back doors? I'm confined to quarters."

"First step," Telzey whispered back, "we move your tapes and stuff to my side. Eulate said under the circumstances it'd be all right if I helped you a little on the tests."

"They can see *your* front and back doors too, dopey!" Gonwil pointed out. "What good will that do?"

"They can't see inside my carport."

"Huh? No!" Gonwil grinned. "The shower window . . ." She looked doubtfully at Chomir. "Can we boost Musclehead through it?"

"We can try. Want to?"

"Ha! When?"

"Right now. Before Eulate realizes you've got a loophole left."

"I should leave her a note," Gonwil remarked. "Something reassuring. I simply *had* to get away for a few days—or suffer a nervous breakdown. . . ."

"Sounds fine," Telzey approved.

"Then, perhaps I should call Malrue and tell her, so . . ."

"Are you out of your mind?"

Gonwil looked reluctant. "You're right. Me being at Pehanron is bad, but going off by myself would be worse. If we didn't agree to wait till she could pick us up outside, she'd be perfectly capable of tipping off Eulate!"

Some minutes later, Telzey came out the back door on her side of the bungalow, dressed for a town trip again. The two Pehanron guards stationed across the traffic lane eyed her as she started towards the enclosed carport, but made no move. They hadn't been instructed to keep watch on Telzey.

Inside the stall and out of their sight, she slid behind the Cloudsplitter's hood, roared the main engine experimentally a few times, glanced up. The shower window already stood open. Chomir's big white head appeared in it now, pointed ears tipped questioningly forwards, broad brow wrinkled in concentration. He had grasped that something unusual was required of him—but what? To look out of Telzey's shower window?

Telzey beckoned.

"Down here, Brainless!"

She couldn't hear Chomir's voice above the noise of the engine, but Chomir's air of well-meaning bewilderment increased. Why, his eyes inquired of Telzey, was Gonwil shoving around at his rear? Then his forepaws came into view, resting on the window sill. Telzey gestured violently, pointing at the ground below the window.

Urged on from in front and behind, Chomir suddenly got the picture. He grinned, lolled out his tongue, sank back, came up and out in a flowing, graceful leap, clearing the window frame by a scant half-inch on all sides. He landed and waved his tail cheerfully at Telzey.

She caught his collar and patted him, while Gonwil, red-faced from her effort to lift more than her own weight in dog straight up, came wriggling through the shower window after him with an overnight bag containing the Finance Eleven tapes and her tapewriter. Telzey slid open the Cloudsplitter's luggage compartment.

A minute later, she turned the little car out into the traffic lane. She had barely been able to shove the luggage compartment's door shut on her two passengers; but they were safely out of sight. The two guards stared thoughtfully after the car as it went gliding down the lane. They could hear the music of a newsviewer program within the duplex. It might be a good half-hour before they got the first proddings of suspicion about Telzey and her aircar.

Coming up to the force-screen exit she'd used in the morning, Telzey snapped the Star Honor Student pass back on her hat. The guards were screening incoming visitors with unusual care today, but students going out were a different matter. They glanced at the pass, at her, waved her through.

As she lifted the car over the crest of the wooded hills north of the college area, a big green airvan veered out of the direction in which it was headed and turned north ahead of her, picking up speed. Fifteen miles on and a few minutes later, Telzey followed the van down to the side of an isolated farm building. En route, there had been a few cautiously questioning knocks from the inside of the luggage compartment. But Telzey ignored them and Gonwil, puzzled, no doubt, about the delay in being let out but trustful as ever, had subsided again.

In the shadow of the farm building, Telzey set the Cloudsplitter down behind the van. Gilas Amberdon clambered out of the front section of the big vehicle and met her beyond hearing range of the luggage compartment.

"Any problems?"

"Not so far," Telzey said. "They're both inside. Has the Kyth Agency found out where the Parlins are?"

"No," Gilas said. "The calls they've made were routed through Orado City but apparently didn't originate there. The chances are they aren't hiding deliberately and will disclose their whereabouts as soon as they hear Gonwil has disappeared from the college."

He studied her a moment. "I realize we're working you a little hard, Telzey. If you take six hours off and catch up on some sleep after we get to the Kyth hideout, it shouldn't make any difference."

She shook her head. "I don't feel particularly tired. And I want to finish up with Chomir. I've got a hunch what he knows will be really important when we get it figured out."

Gilas considered. "All right. Dasinger would like to have that. We'll be there shortly. You'll get separate quarters as you specified—close enough to Gonwil and Chomir to let you work your mental witchcraft on them. And you'll be completely undisturbed."

"That will be fine," Telzey said.

Her father smiled. "Then let's go!"

He started towards the front of the van. Telzey walked back to the Cloudsplitter and slipped into her seat. Half a minute later, the end of the van opened out. She slid the car up and inside and shut off its engine. Benches lined this section of the vehicle. Aside from that, it was empty.

The loading door slammed shut again and the section lights came on overhead. Telzey waited until she felt the van lift creakily into the air. Then she opened the luggage compartment and let her rumpled passengers emerge.

"What in the world," Gonwil inquired bewilderedly, straightening up and staring around as Chomir eased himself out of the Cloudsplitter behind her, "are we doing in this thing?"

"Being scooted off to a safe hiding place," Telzey said. "That was all arranged for in advance."

"Arranged for—safe . . ." Gonwil's voice was strained. "Telzey! Whose idea was this?"

"The Bank of Rienne's."

The room they'd put her in here, Gonwil acknowledged, was, though not very large, comfortable and attractively furnished. If, nevertheless, it gave her a somewhat oppressive feeling of being imprisoned, that could be attributed to the fact that it was windowless and lacked means of outside communication.

The only way to leave would be to go through a short corridor and open a door at the far end, which let into an office where a number of

people were working. So she couldn't have
slipped away unnoticed, but there was no reason
to think the people in the office would try to
detain her if she did decide to leave. She'd simply
been asked to stay here long enough to let the
Bank of Rienne determine whether there could be
any sinister significance to the appearance of the
inquisitive strangers at the Tayun consulate that
morning.

During the brief ride in the airvan, Telzey had
explained that the bank felt its investigation
would be greatly simplified if it could be carried
out in complete secrecy. Pehanron College did
not seem a safe place to leave Gonwil if somebody did intend to harm her; and to avoid revealing that it was taking a hand in the matter, the
bank had called on Telzey, through her father, to
spirit Gonwil quietly away from the campus.

Allowing for the fact, that, at the moment,
everybody appeared obsessed by the notion
that Tayun vendettists were after her, it wasn't
an unreasonable explanation. The Bank of
Rienne did have some grounds to consider itself
responsible for her here. "But why," Gonwil had
asked, "didn't you tell me all this before we
left?"

"Would you have come along if I had?" Telzey
said.

Gonwil reflected and admitted that she probably wouldn't have come along. She didn't want
to appear ungrateful; and she had now begun to
feel the first touches of apprehension. When so
many people, including Telzey's eminently practical father, were indicating concern for her
safety, the possibility couldn't be denied that

there was more to the old vendettist stories than she'd been willing to believe. Cousin Malrue, after all, was no fool; perhaps she had done Malrue an inexcusable injustice in belittling her warnings! Gonwil had only a vague idea of the methods a capable murderer might use to reach his victim; but it was generally accepted that he had a frightening array of weapons to choose from, and that every precaution must be taken in such situations.

At any rate, she was perfectly safe here. The door to the room was locked; she had one key to it, Gilas Amberdon another. She was to let no one but Telzey in, and to make sure that no one else attempted to enter, Chomir was on guard in the corridor outside. It was comfortable to remember now that if Chomir was no shining light when it came to the standard doggy tricks, the protection of a human being was as solidly stamped into his nature as the gory skills of the arena. While he could move, only Gonwil or Telzey would open that door until one of them convinced him he could stop being a watchdog again.

And now that she was alone, Gonwil thought, there was something she should take care of promptly.

Opening the overnight bag she had taken from the college, she arranged her study materials on a desk shelf, then brought out the miniature camouflaged communicator which had come with the mail in the morning. She had dropped Junior's unwanted token of affection in with the tapewriter and other items, intending to show it to Telzey later on.

She studied the tiny instrument a moment,

pensively biting her lip. There had been no opportunity to tell Telzey about it, so no one here knew she had the thing. The lack of communicators among the room furnishings might mean that they'd rather she didn't send messages outside. But they hadn't said so.

And it seemed only fair to send Malrue a reassuring word through Junior now. There would be no need to mention the Bank of Rienne's investigation. She could tell Junior a very harmless story, one designed only to keep his mother from becoming completely distraught when she heard from Pehanron College that Gonwil had chosen to disappear.

Gonwil glanced back a moment at the door. Then she placed the communicator in the palm of her left hand, and shifted the emerald arrowhead in its cover design a quarter turn to the right. That, according to the instructions which had come with it, made it ready for use. She placed it on the desk shelf, and pressed down with a fingertip on the golden pinhead stud in the center of the cover.

A slender fan of golden light sprang up and out from around the rim of the communicator, trembled, widened, and held steady. It was perhaps three feet across, not much over two high, slightly concave. This was the vision screen.

Now, if she turned the little arrowhead to the third notch, and Junior's communicator was set to receive, he should hear her signal.

Some ten or twelve seconds passed. Then Rodel Parlin the Twelfth's handsome, narrow face was suddenly there in the fan-shaped golden light screen before her.

"Well, *at last!*" he exclaimed. "I've been trying to call you but . . ."

"I didn't switch it on until just now," Gonwil admitted.

"Busy as all that with your tests?" Junior's gaze shifted past her, went around the room. "What's this?" he inquired. "Did Pehanron actually change your quarters because of the vendettist scare?"

So the Parlins hadn't been told she was gone. Gonwil smiled.

"Pehanron didn't!" she said. "I did. The fuss was getting too much for my nerves, so I sneaked out!"

For a moment, Junior looked startled. "You've left the college?"

"Uh-huh."

"Well, I . . . where are you now?"

"I'm not telling anybody," she said. "I've gone underground, so to speak, and I intend to stay out of sight until the thing blows over."

"Well, uh, Malrue . . ."

"I know. That's why I called the first chance I had. I don't want Malrue to worry unnecessarily, so you tell her I'm in a perfectly safe place. Nobody here knows me, so nobody—including vendettists—can find out where I've gone. Tell Malrue I'm being very careful, and whenever you all decide there's no more danger, I'll come out again."

Junior studied her, frowning doubtfully.

"Malrue," he observed, "isn't going to like that very much!"

"Yes, I . . . just a moment!" Gonwil turned towards the door. Sounds of scratching came from it, then a deep whine. "That's Chomir! He heard us talking, and I'd better let him in before he arouses the neighborhood. It's difficult enough to be inconspicuous with *him* around!"

"I can imagine."

Gonwil unlocked the door and opened it partly, glancing up the hall as Chomir slid through into the room, ears pricked. The door at the far end of the corridor was closed; he hadn't been heard in the office. She locked the door quietly again. Chomir stared for an instant at the image in the view-field, took a sniff at the air to confirm that while he'd heard Junior's voice, Junior was not physically present. Chomir was familiar with the phenomenon of communicator screens and the ghosts that periodically appeared in them. Satisfied, he sat down beside the door.

"I was wondering whether you'd left him behind," Junior remarked as Gonwil came back.

"Oh, I wouldn't do that to Chomir! About Malrue . . ."

He grinned. "I know! She does carry on rather badly at times like this! I'll be tactful in what I tell her."

"Thanks," Gonwil said gratefully. "I wouldn't want her to feel that I'm avoiding her in particular. But would you please not tell her about sending me a personal communicator? Say I was just using a regular ComWeb in making this call. Otherwise, she'd want to argue me out of this, and I'd hate to have to refuse her."

"You can depend on me. When will you call again?"

"Sometime early tomorrow?"

"I'll be waiting." He turned his head to the left, appeared to listen. Then he looked back at her.

"I believe I hear Malrue coming," he said quietly. "Goodby, Gonwil!"

" 'By, Junior!"

His face vanished. Still smiling, Gonwil bent over the communicator, searching for the pinhead stud. Junior had been on his best behavior this time; she was very glad she'd decided to make the call.

She pushed down the stud, and the light screen disappeared.

From the far end of the corridor outside came the sound of a violently slammed door.

Startled, Gonwil swung about. Footsteps were pounding up the short corridor now, but she wasn't aware of them. She stood dead-still, staring.

The white shape crouched across the room, ears back and down, huge teeth bared, could hardly be recognized as Chomir. He might have been listening to the approaching steps. But then the snarling head moved. The eyes found Gonwil, and instantly he was coming towards her in a flat, long spring, jaws wide.

As she watched Chomir move off beside Gonwil through the entrance tunnel to the Kyth hideout where the airvan had stopped, Telzey put out a tentative probe towards him.

This time, she was inside the dog's mind at once and so definitely that she could sense him striding along and the touch of the hard flooring beneath his pad. Satisfied, she withdrew. The contacts established during the night's work hadn't faded; she could resume her investigation immediately.

Left alone in the room reserved for her, less than fifty feet from the one to which they had conducted Gonwil, Telzey settled into an armchair and closed her eyes. Chomir still seemed to be moving about, but that made no difference. At this stage, she could work below his awareness without disturbing him or interfering with his activities.

She picked up the familiar memory chains within seconds, and then hesitated. Something had changed here. There was a sense of being drawn quietly away from the memories towards another area of mind.

She didn't know what it meant. But since psi seemed sometimes to work independently on problems in which one was involved, this might turn out to be a short-cut to the information for which she had been digging throughout the night. Telzey let herself shift in the indicated direction. There was a momentary odd feeling of sinking, then of having made a transition, of being somewhere else.

And it had been a short-cut. This was an aspect of mind she hadn't explored before, but it wasn't difficult to understand. A computer's processes might have presented a somewhat similar pattern: impersonal, unaware, enormously detailed and busy. Its universe was the living animal body that generated it, and its function was essentially to see to it that its universe remained physically in good operating condition. As Telzey grasped that, her attention shifted once more—now to a disturbance point in the Chomir universe. Something was wrong there. The body-mind knew it was wrong but was unable to do anything about it.

Telzey studied the disturbance point absorbedly. Suddenly its meaning became clear; and then she knew this was the information she had come to find. And it was very ugly and disturbing information.

She opened her eyes. Her thoughts seemed sluggish, and for some seconds the room looked hazy and blurred about her. Then, as the body-mind patterns faded from her awareness, she discovered she was back in the ordinary sort of contact with Chomir—very clear, strong contact. She had a feeling of catching Gonwil's voice impressions through him.

The voice impressions ended. There was a moment's pause. A sharp surge of uneasiness passed through Chomir.

What did that . . .

Telzey felt the blood drain from her face as she scrambled abruptly out of the chair, reaching for the room communicator. Then her breath caught. She stopped in mid-motion, stood swaying. Electric shivers were racing over her skin. The air seemed to tingle. Psi energy was building up swiftly, oppressively; and she was its focal point.

Fury swept towards her, mindless, elemental, like a roaring wind. She seemed to move, and the room flickered out of existence. Something raged, and about her spun a disk of noise, of shock-distorted faces, of monstrously straining muscles. She moved again, and everything was still and clear.

She was looking into another room, a day-bright room where a man in a yellow suit stood beside a window, studying the small device he held in one hand. Beyond the window, sunlit parkland stretched away in long, rising slopes; and in the far distance, high on the slopes, was the glassy glitter of a familiar cluster of buildings.

Something appeared to startle the man. His face turned quickly towards her; and as she registered the details of the sharp features and wispy blond mustache, his eyes became round, white-rimmed holes of intense fright.

The room vanished. Then there was one more sensation, remarkably like being slammed several times on top of the head by a giant fist; and a wave of blackness rolled over Telzey and swept her down. . . .

XI

"OH, HE'S admitted it, all right!" Dasinger said, frowning at the solidopic of the man with the thin blond mustache. "In fact, as soon as he was told why he'd been picked up, he became anxious to spill everything he knew. But his confession isn't going to be of much use against the Parlins."

"Why not?" Telzey asked.

"Because one thing he didn't know was who his employers were." The detective nodded at the tapeviewer he'd put on the table before her. "You can get the details from the report faster than I could give them to you. I have some questions myself, by the way."

"What about, Mr. Dasinger?"

"It seems," Dasinger said, "that when you sensed the dog was turning on Miss Lodis, you did three things almost simultaneously. You pinned the animal down in some manner . . ."

Telzey nodded. "I kept locking his muscles on him. That's what it felt like."

"That's what it looked like," Dasinger agreed. "When we got into the room, he was twisting around on the floor and seemed unable to open his jaws. Even so, he gave us one of the most startling demonstrations of animal athletics I've seen. It was a good half minute before somebody could line up on him long enough to feed him a stunner! Besides keeping Miss Lodis from getting killed in there, you've probably also saved the lives of three or four of my men ... a detail which the Kyth Agency will remember. Now, as you clamped down on the dog, you also blasted a telepathic warning to your father to let us know Miss Lodis needed immediate help."

"Uh-huh. I didn't realize till afterwards I'd done it though."

"Meanwhile again," Dasinger said, indicating the solidopic, "you were putting in a personal appearance in the city of Beale, a good thousand miles away, in the room where this gentleman was operating the instrument which was supposed to be accomplishing the murder of Miss Lodis."

Telzey hesitated, said "I seemed to be there, for just a few moments. He looked scared to death, and I was wondering if he could see me."

"He saw something," the detective said, "and he's described it. The description fits you. The fellow hadn't been told who the intended victim was, and up to that moment he hadn't particularly cared. But his conclusion was that the accusing wraith of the person he'd just helped murder had appeared in the room. That left his nerves in pitiable condition, I'm happy to say, and has made him very easy to handle.

"On the other hand, of course, this experience, again limits his usefulness to us. We don't want him to talk about it, because we don't want to start speculations about you personally."

"No, I see."

"I'm assuming," Dasinger went on, "that it was also a rather unusual experience as far as you were concerned. If you could do that kind of thing regularly, you obviously wouldn't need assistance in solving Miss Lodis's problems."

Telzey hesitated. It seemed to her there had been, in that instant, a completely improbable combination of factors, resulting in something like a psychic explosion. The fury pouring out of the dog's mind might have set it off; and she'd been simply involved in it then, doing what she urgently wished to do, but not at all controlling the fact that she was doing it, or how it was done.

It had worked out very well; Gonwil and some other people and Chomir would be dead now if it hadn't happened in just that way. But she wasn't eager for another experience of the kind. The next time it might as easily work out very badly.

She explained it to Dasinger as well as she could. He listened attentively, frowning now and then. At last he said, "Perhaps you'd better look over the report on Mrs. Parlin's hired assassin. Then I'll explain what the situation seems to be now."

Whether or not she'd actually gone to Beale in any physical sense during those few seconds, she hadn't relaxed her mental hold on Chomir while she was doing it. And while that had saved lives, it had one drawback. When someone finally poured a stunblast into the big dog, the connection between them was strong enough to transmit echoes of the pounding shock to her brain. It knocked her out, but since she hadn't absorbed the stunner physically the Kyth operatives brought her around again within minutes.

Then, after she'd barely finished giving them the description of the man in Beale, along with the information that Pehanron College could be seen at a certain angle, roughly five miles away, from the window of the room he was in, some well-meaning character slipped her a sedative in a glass of water without stopping to inquire whether she wanted one. Conceivably, she appeared a little feverish and wild-eyed, as who wouldn't under such circumstances? At any rate, she was unconscious again before she knew what had occurred.

The next time she awoke, eighteen hours had passed and she was in one of the cabins of the spacecruiser maintained by the Bank of Rienne for Gilas Amberdon's use. They were in space, though not far from Orado; she was in bed, and a large woman in a nurse's uniform was sitting next to the bed. The large woman informed her firmly that she would remain in bed until Mr. Amberdon's physician had come out from the planet to examine her again. Telzey, with equal firmness, dismissed the nurse from the cabin, got dressed, and went out to learn what had taken place meanwhile.

In the passage she encountered Dasinger, looking harried. The Kyth chief told her Gilas and Gonwil were in the communications cabin, involved in a ship-to-planet conference with Rienne's legal department, and offered to bring her up-to-date.

It appeared that the Kyth operatives dis-

patched to Beale early yesterday to look for
Chomir's menacing stranger had picked up
their quarry very shortly after receiving Telzey's
description of him and of the area where he
could be found. It had been a lucky break; he was
on his way to the nearest spaceport by then. They
learned his name was Vingarran, that he was a
native of Askanam where he had some reputa-
tion as a trainer of arena animals; and that he had
received an extremely attractive financial offer to
come to Orado and apply for work in a high-
priced veterinarian establishment in the town of
Beale, where he presently would carry out a
specific assignment. The vet's was the place
where Gonwil left Chomir regularly for his
check-up and shots.

In due time, acting on instructions, Vingarran
drugged the big dog and planted a device in his
brain, of a type sometimes used on Askanam
fighting animals when the betting was heavy. Essentially, it was a telecontrolled miniature instrument which produced at will anything from
a brief surge of anger to sustained insane fury.
Animals so manipulated rarely lost a fight in
which they were otherwise evenly matched, and
cheating was almost impossible to prove because
the instrument dissolved itself after fulfilling its
function, leaving only microscopic scars in the
brain tissue. After arousing Chomir from his
drugged sleep, Vingarran tested his device and
found it in good working order.

Some months passed without further action.
Then Vingarran received instructions to check
the dog's response again at the first available opportunity. He had done this from an aircar while

Gonwil and Chomir were on one of their customary hikes in the hills. Following his report that
the dog had reacted satisfactorily to minimum
stimulus, he was told to wait for a signal which
would be his cue to employ the instrument at full
output for a period of five minutes, after which it
was to be destroyed in the usual manner. This
would conclude the services for which he had
been hired.

Vingarran had no real doubt that at least one
person would be slaughtered by the white hound
during those five minutes—that this was calculated murder. But he was being paid well enough
to tell himself that what happened when he
pushed down the control plunger was not his responsibility but that of his employers. And a few
hours later, he would be on his way back to Askanam, and need never hear what the result of
his action had been.

The vendettist scare at the Tayun consulate
followed. Professionally, Dasinger regarded it as
an unnecessary touch; the authorities investigating Gonwil's death were certain to conclude that
her giant pet had gone berserk and destroyed her
with the savagery that could be expected of a
fierce fighting breed. But the Parlins evidently
preferred to have an alternate explanation ready
if there were any questions. When Junior established that Gonwil was for the moment alone in a
locked room with the dog, the signal was flashed
to Vingarran to carry out his orders.

It was a complete picture, except for the unfortunate fact mentioned by Dasinger; the man from
Askanam simply did not have the faintest notion
who had hired him or from what source his pay

had come. He did not know the Parlins, had never seen one of them or heard their voices. He had been told what to do through the impersonal medium of a telewriter. The Kyth Agency would keep him under wraps; but there seemed to be no practical possibility of using him as a witness.

Telzey asked, "Does Malrue know it didn't work . . . That Gonwil didn't get killed or hurt?"

"She knows she couldn't have been hurt seriously enough to incapacitate her," Dasinger said. "She also knows we're aware it was attempted murder, and who was behind it."

"Oh . . . how did she find out?"

"Indirectly, from us. It couldn't very well be avoided. Miss Lodis responded in a very level-headed manner after the situation had been explained to her and she was over the first feeling of shock about it. Junior's call immediately before the dog's attack fitted in too well with the rest of it to let her retain doubts about Mrs. Parlin's guilt. She agreed at once to apply to become the legal ward of the Bank of Rienne. That made it possible for us to act freely on her behalf; but when her guardians on Tayun were notified of the move, it told them, of course, that Mrs. Parlin's plans had miscarried and that they themselves were suspected of complicity. They must have warned the Parlins immediately."

"They didn't argue about the bank becoming Gonwil's guardian?" Telzey asked.

"No. The thing had come into the open, and they realized it. Which is why we're in space. It's one way to make sure Miss Lodis is safe for the moment."

Telzey had a sinking feeling. "For the moment? You don't think the Parlins might give up?"

The detective shook his head. "Not after what we've learned about Mrs. Parlin. She's playing for high stakes here. She's planned for years to get Miss Lodis's share of the company in her hands, and she won't stop now simply because it can't be done quietly any more. It's reasonable to suppose she won't be involved in future murder attempts herself, since that might get her into trouble. But all she has to do is set enough price on your friend's head to attract professional sharpshooters. From now on, that's what we'll have to look for."

"But then . . ." Telzey paused. "Then what are we going to do?"

"At present," Dasinger said, "the matter is in the hands of Rienne's attorneys. They'll investigate all legal possibilities. That may take some days. That the Parlins are anticipating moves in that area is indicated by the fact that they've assembled a legal staff of their own. But I don't think they're greatly worried by that approach."

He considered, added, "We'll see what develops. I haven't, of course, suggested to Miss Lodis that we might turn the situation into a registered private war. She's still pretty badly shaken up by the treachery of the Parlin family, and particularly of Mrs. Parlin."

"You're waiting to let her find out there's nothing else she can do?" Telzey asked.

"Perhaps I am."

Telzey shook her head.

"She still won't do it," she said. "Not if it means killing Malrue Parlin."

"It would mean that," Dasinger said. "We might simply frighten the lady into backing off. But it wouldn't settle anything. Miss Lodis would never be safe from her again. Unless, of course, she simply turned her stock over to Mrs. Parlin, on Mrs. Parlin's terms."

"She'd sooner do that," Telzey said. Her skin was crawling.

"Would you like to see it happen?"

"No," Telzey admitted.

"Well, let's let it rest there," Dasinger said. "The lawyers may come up with something. Incidentally, you might see what you can do about Chomir, Miss Amberdon. He's in rather bad shape."

"I thought he was all right again!" Telzey said, startled.

"Oh, the stunner didn't harm him, of course. I'll take you there, and we'll see what you think. If it weren't ridiculous, I'd say he was suffering from a psychotic collapse, brought on by guilt. When Miss Lodis tries to talk to him, he looks away and pretends she isn't there."

Dasinger's diagnosis was accurate enough. Telzey found Chomir lost in a black stew of despondency. His memory of what had occurred after the rage stimulus began to blaze through his brain was a horrid muddle of impressions; but he knew the evil stranger had been nearby in his insubstantial way, and that he, Chomir, had done dreadful things. And the stranger had again escaped. Chomir felt miserably unable to face Gonwil. . . .

It might be possible actually to delete unpleasant memories from a mind, but Telzey hadn't found out how to do it. However, it wasn't difficult to blur out some remembered event until it was barely discernible, and then to shift over other little chunks of memory and imagination from here and there and work them together until, so far as the owner of the mind was concerned, a completely new memory had been created in place of the obscured one.

After about an hour and a half, Chomir wasn't even aware that he had been glooming about something a short while ago. When Gonwil showed up, having heard that Telzey had awakened and was with the dog, he was plainly back to normal behavior.

Other problems, unfortunately, weren't going to be as simple to solve. Gonwil felt that after the first round of conferences with the Bank of Rienne's legal department the lawyers' initial attitude of cautious optimism was beginning to fade. The possibility of bringing charges against the Parlin family in Federation court had been ruled out almost at once. A conviction could be obtained against Vingarran; but not—while their mind-blocks protected them from subjective probes—against the Parlins. And there was, of course, no point in prosecuting Vingarran alone. It would be preferable to leave the Parlins unaware for the present of what had happened to their hireling from Askanam.

Rienne's attorneys regarded the prospects of a Transcluster Finance ethics hearing as somewhat more promising, though one would have to give detailed consideration to the evidence which might be presented for verification before forming a definite conclusion. If it could be shown in an ethics hearing that the Parlins had planned the murder of a business associate for profit, the results would be almost as satisfactory as a court conviction. Transcluster's adjudicators could not route them through Rehabilitation, but they could order the confiscation of their holdings in Lodis Associates and block them for life from again playing an open role in the Hub's financial world.

The alternative—not infrequently chosen in such cases—was voluntary Rehabilitation. Rienne's attorneys' hope was that some connection could be established between the Parlin family and the death of various other members of Lodis Associates who had been known to be in opposition to them. Added to evidence obtained from the attempted murder of Gonwil Lodis, it might give them a case, though a most difficult one to prepare. The Verifier gave no consideration to probabilities and did not evaluate evidence aside from reporting that the mental information made available to it had showed a specific claim to be true or false, or had failed to show either its truth or falsity. Any facts obtained must therefore be carefully arranged into a pattern which would condemn the Parlins when confirmed by the mind-machine. And that would take time.

The truth of the matter probably was, Telzey thought, that a Verifier, or its operators, was capable of sizing up the merits of a case almost as soon as an ethics hearing began—if her calculations about the function and potential of the Psychology Service's machines had come anywhere near the mark. But in dealing with them it could make no practical difference, because they wouldn't admit to seeing more than they were supposed to see, even if it meant letting a hearing end in favor of someone like Malrue Parlin. Of course, they couldn't have maintained their big secret otherwise. But it seemed very unlikely that the lawyers were going to dig up something in Malrue's past which could coax a damaging report out of the machine. Malrue would have been as cautious about leaving no direct evidence of earlier murderous activities as she had been in her plans for Gonwil.

The lawyers obviously weren't counting on it either. Another matter they would investigate was the possibility of breaking the clause which effectively prevented Gonwil from selling her stock in Lodis Associates to anyone but another associate. If the Bank of Rienne acquired the stock, it would put an end to Malrue's maneuverings. At the moment, however, it looked as if six or eight years of wrangling in Tayun courts might be required to force a favorable decision on that point.

All in all, Telzey reflected, Dasinger's pessimism was beginning to appear justified. And the mere fact that they were at present confined to the spacecruiser was an intimation of what it could be like to live for years on guard against some unknown assassin's stroke, or hiding somewhere, shut off from normal existence. Dasinger might, as a matter of fact, have arranged the temporary retreat from Orado in part to demonstrate just that.

When they gathered for dinner, she learned that Pehanron College, after being privately briefed by

Rienne officials on the current state of affairs, had sent word it was co-operating by placing both Gonwil and Telzey on technical sick leave for as long as might be necessary.

That seemed somehow the most decisive move of the day.

After dinner, she retired early to her cabin. It was possible, as Dasinger had suggested, that the attorneys would still come up with a practical solution. But one clearly couldn't depend on it.

She sent out a threat of thought for Chomir, located him in the cruiser's lounge with Gonwil and Gilas, and slipped back into his mind. It was as easy now as walking into a house to which one owned the key. When ship-night was sounded an hour or so later, she was with him as he followed Gonwil to her cabin. And quite a little later again, she knew Gonwil finally had found troubled sleep.

Telzey withdrew from Chomir and put out the drifting telepathic probe which by and by would touch one of Gonwil's sleeping thoughts and through it establish the first insubstantial bridge between their minds. Then, in a day or two, she would be in control of Gonwil's mental activities, in the same unsuspected and untraceable way and as completely, as she was of Chomir's.

She felt uncomfortable about it. It hadn't disturbed her at all to tap the minds of strangers, just to see what was in there and to experiment a little. Intruding on the private thoughts of a friend, secretly and uninvited, somehow seemed a very different matter.

But the way things appeared to be going made it necessary now.

It was a week before the subject of registering for a private war came up again; and now it wasn't Dasinger's suggestion. The bank's attorneys recommended the move, though with obvious reluctance, to Gilas and Gonwil, as an apparently necessary one if Mrs. Parlin's designs on Gonwil's share in Lodis Associates were to be checked.

By then, nobody, including Gonwil, was really surprised to hear of it. It had been a frustrating week for the legal staff. While they felt they weren't at the end of their resources, it was clear that Malrue Parlin had been prepared for years to face a day of reckoning. The investigators on Tayun reported many suspicious circumstances about her activities, but produced no scrap of evidence to connect the Parlins to them. Malrue had few allies with whom she had worked directly; and all of them had protected themselves as carefully as she did.

Other approaches had brought equally negative results. The rule barring members of Lodis Associates from selling shares to outsiders before their fellows were given an opportunity to purchase them at a prohibitively low price was found to be backed in full by Tayun law. While Gonwil was still a child, the rule could have been set aside with relative ease, but there appeared to be no way around it now that she would be a legally responsible adult within a few months. The minor shareholders in the concern had declined offers of her stock at something approximating its present value, and indicated they would have no interest in it at any price. They clearly didn't intend to get into Malrue Parlin's game.

The Parlins were still on Orado, equipped with a formidable bodyguard and an equally formidable corps of lawyers, both imports from Tayun who evidently had preceded Malrue and her husband here, to be brought into action if needed. But Malrue had made no immediate moves. She might be satisfied to let Gonwil's supporters find out for themselves that her legal position was unassailable.

Telzey had remained a detached observer of these developments, realizing they were running uncomfortably close to Dasinger's predictions. She was giving most of her time to Gonwil. Her previous investigations of human minds had been brief and directed as a rule to specific details, but she felt there was reason to be very careful here.

What was going on inside Gonwil's blond head nowadays wasn't good. Harm had been done, and Telzey was afraid to tamper with the results, to attempt the role of healer. It wasn't a simple matter of patching up a few memories as with Chomir; there was too much she didn't understand. Gonwil would have to do her own healing, at least at the start, and to an extent she was doing it. During the first day or two, her thoughts had a numbed quality to them. Outwardly she acquiesced in everything, was polite, smiled occasionally. But something had been shattered; and she was waiting to see what the people about her would do, how they intended to put all the pieces together again. When she thought of Cousin Malrue's treachery, it was in a puzzled, childish manner.

Then, gradually, she began to understand that

he pieces weren't simply going to be put together again now. This ugliness could go on indefinitely, excluding her meanwhile from normal human life.

The realization woke Gonwil up. Until then,
most of the details of the situation about her had
been blurred and without much meaning. Now
she started to look them over carefully, and they
became obvious enough.

The efforts of Rienne's lawyers to find a satisfactory solution had begun to bog down because
this was a matter which the Federation's laws
did not adequately cover. She had been one of
the Hub's favored and pampered children, but in
part that was now the reason she was being
forced towards the edge of a no man's land where
survival depended on oneself and one's friends.
Unless something quite unexpected happened,
she would soon have to decide what the future
would be like.

The thought startled her, but she accepted it.
There was a boy in the Federation Navy, a cadet
she'd met the previous summer, who played a
part in her considerations. So did Telzey, and
Dasinger and his agency, and Malrue and her
husband and Junior, and the group of professional gunmen they'd brought in from Tayun to
be their bodyguards. All of them would be affected in one way or another by what she agreed
to. She must be very careful to make no mistakes.

Gonwil, seen directly in her reflections and
shifts of feeling now that she'd snapped out of
the numbed shock, seemed more likeable than
ever to Telzey. But she didn't like at all what was
almost surely coming.

It came. Mainly perhaps for the purpose of having it on record, Rienne's legal department had notified the Parlins' lawyers in Orado City that Miss Lodis desired to dispose of her stock in Lodis Associates. A reply two days later stated that Malrue Parlin, though painfully affected by Miss Lodis's estrangement from herself and her family, was willing to take over the stock. She was not unmindful of her right to purchase at the original value, but would pay twice that, solely to accommodate Miss Lodis.

In Telzey's opinion, the legal department flipped when it read the reply. It had, of course, been putting up with a good deal during the week. It called promptly for a planet-to-ship general conference, and pointed out that the sum Malrue offered was approximately a tenth of the real value of Gonwil's share in the concern. In view of the fact that an attempt to murder Miss Lodis already had been made, Mrs. Parlin's reply must be considered not a bona fide offer but a form of extortion. A threat was implied.

However, Mrs. Parlin might be showing more confidence than she felt. If violence again entered the picture, she was now not invulnerable. To some extent, at least, she was bluffing. To counter the bluff, she should be shown unmistakably that Miss Lodis was determined to defend herself and her interests by whatever means were necessary.

The legal department's advice at this point must be to have Miss Lodis register the fact that against her wishes she had become involved in a private war with the Parlin family, and that she was appointing the Kyth Agency to act as her

agent in this affair. The events and investigations
of the past week provided more than sufficient
grounds for the registration, and its purpose
would go beyond making it clear to the Parlins
that from now on they would be in jeopardy no
less than Miss Lodis. It had been discovered that
while the rule which prevented the sale of Lodis
Associates stock outside the concern could not
be broken in court, it could be rescinded by a
two-thirds majority vote of the shareholders, and
Miss Lodis and the Parlin family between them
controlled more than two thirds of the stock. No
doubt, forcible means would be required to persuade the Parlins to agree to the action, but the
agreement would be valid if obtained in that
manner under the necessities of a registered private war. Miss Lodis could then sell her shares at
full value to the Bank of Rienne or a similar in-
stitution, which would end the Parlins' efforts to
obtain them, and take her out of danger.

Registration, the legal department added, was
serious matter, of course, and Miss Lodis should
give it sufficient thought before deciding to sign
the application they had prepared. On the other
hand, it might be best not to delay more than a day
or two. The Parlins' attitude showed she would be
safe only so long as they did not know where she
was.

"Has she discussed it with you?" Dasinger
asked.

Telzey looked at him irritably. Her nerves had
been on edge since the conference ended. Things
had taken a very unsatisfactory turn. If Malrue
Parlin would only drop dead!

She shook her head. "She's been in her room. We haven't talked about it yet."

Dasinger studied her face. "Your father and I," he remarked, "aren't entirely happy about having her register for a private war."

"Why not? I thought you . . ."

He nodded. "I know. But in view of what you said, I've been watching her, and I'm inclined to agree now that she might be too civilized for such methods. It's a pleasant trait, though it's been known to be a suicidal one."

He hesitated, went on. "Aside from that, a private war is simply the only practical answer now. And it would be best to act at once while the Parlin family is together and on Orado. If we wait till they scatter, it will be the devil's own job roping them in again. I think I can guarantee that none of the three will be physically injured. As for Miss Lodis's feelings about it, we—your father and I—assume that your ability to handle emotional disturbances isn't limited to animals."

Telzey shifted uneasily in her chair. Her skull felt tight; she might be getting a headache. She wondered why she didn't tell the detective to stop worrying. Gonwil had found her own solution before the conference was over. She wouldn't authorize a private war for any purpose. No matter how expertly it was handled, somebody was going to get killed when two bands of armed men came into conflict, and she didn't want the responsibility for it.

Neither did she want to run and hide for years to keep Malrue from having her killed. The money wasn't worth it.

So the logical answer was to accept Malrue's

offer and let her have the stock and control of
Lodis Associates. Gonwil could get along very
well without it. And she wouldn't have con-
sented to someone's death to keep it.

Gonwil didn't know why she hadn't told them
that at the conference, though Telzey did. Gonwil had intended to speak, then suddenly forgotten her intention. Another few hours, Telzey had
thought, to make sure there wasn't some answer
as logical as surrender but more satisfactory. A
private war didn't happen to be it.

She realized she'd said something because
Dasinger was continuing. Malrue Parlin appeared to have played into their hands through
overconfidence. . . .

That, Telzey thought, was where they were
wrong. The past few days had showed her things
about Gonwil which had remained partly unre-
vealed in two years of friendship. But a shrewd
and purposeful observer like Malrue Parlin,
knowing Gonwil since her year of birth, would
be aware of them.

Gonwil didn't simply have a prejudice against
violence; she was incapable of it. Malrue knew it.
It would have suited her best if Gonwil died in a
manner which didn't look like murder, or at least
didn't turn suspicion on the Parlins. But she
needn't feel any concern because she had failed
in that. The shock of knowing that murder had
been tried, of realizing that more of that kind of
thing would be necessary if Malrue was to be
stopped, would be enough. It wasn't so much
fear as revulsion—a need to draw away from the
ugly business. Gonwil would give in.

Cousin Malrue hadn't been overconfident. She'd simply known exactly what would happen.

Anger was an uncomfortable thing. Telzey's skin crawled with it. Dasinger asked a question, and she said something which must have made sense because he smiled briefly and nodded, and went on talking. But she didn't remember then what the question had been or what she had replied. For a moment, her vision blurred and the room seemed to rock. It was almost as if she'd heard Malrue Parlin laughing nearby, already savoring her victory, sure she'd placed herself beyond reprisal.

Malrue winning out over Gonwil like that was a thing that couldn't be accepted; and she'd prevented Gonwil from admitting it. But she was unable to do what Gilas and Dasinger expected now—change Gonwil's opinions around until she agreed cheerfully to whatever arrangements they made. And if people got killed during her private war, well, that would be too bad but it had been made inevitable by the Parlins' criminal greed and the Federation's sloppy laws, hadn't it.

It was quite possible to do, but not by changing a few of Gonwil's civilized though unrealistic attitudes. It could be done only by twisting and distorting whatever was Gonwil. And that wouldn't ever be undone again.

Malrue laughed once more, mocking and triumphant, and it was like pulling a trigger. Dasinger still seemed to be talking somewhere, but the room had shifted and disappeared. She was in a darkness where laughter echoed and black electric gusts swirled heavily around her, looking out at a tall, handsome woman in a group of people. Behind Telzey, something rose swiftly, black and towering like a wave about to break, curving over towards the woman.

Then there was a violent, wrenching effort of some sort.

She was back in her chair, shaking, her face wet with sweat, with a sense of having stopped at the last possible instant. The room swam past her eyes and it seemed, as something she half-recalled, that Dasinger had just left, closing the door behind him, still unaware that anything out of the ordinary was going on with Telzey. But she wasn't completely alone. A miniature figure of the Psionic Cop hovered before her face, gesticulating and mouthing inaudible protests. He looked ridiculous, Telzey thought. She made a giggling noise at him, shaking her head, and he vanished.

She got out a handkerchief and dabbed at her face. She felt giddy and weak. Dasinger had noticed nothing, so she hadn't really gone anywhere physically, even for a second or two. Nevertheless, on Orado half a million miles away, Malrue Parlin, laughing and confident in a group of friends or guests, had been only moments from invisible, untraceable death. If that wave of silent energy had reached her, she would have groaned and staggered and fallen, while her companions stared, sensing nothing.

What created the wave? She hadn't done it consciously—but it would be a good thing to remember not to let hot, foggy anger become mixed with a psi impulse again! She wasn't Gonwil, but to put somebody to death in that manner would be rather horrid. And the weakness in her suggested that it mightn't be healthy for the psi who did it, unless he had something like the equipment of that alien in the university's habitat museum.

At any rate, her anger had spent itself now. The necessity of doing something to prevent Gonwil's surrender remained.

And then it occurred to Telzey how it might be done.

She considered a minute or two, and put out a search-thought for Chomir, touched his mind and slipped into it. Groping about briefly, she picked up the artificial memory section she'd installed to cover the disturbing events in the Kyth Agency's hideout.

She had worked the section in rather carefully. Even if Chomir had been a fairly introspective and alert human being, he might very well have accepted it as what had happened. But it wasn't likely that an intruding telepath who studied the section at all closely would be fooled. She certainly wouldn't be. It seemed a practical impossibility to invest artificial memories with the multitudinous, interconnected, coherent detail which characterized actual events. Neither was the buried original memory really buried when one began to search for it. It could be brought out and developed again.

And if such constructions couldn't fool her, could they fool a high-powered psionic mind-reading device, built for the specific purpose of finding out what somebody really thought, believed and remembered . . . such as Transcluster Finance's verifying machines?

They couldn't of course.

Telzey sat still again a while, biting her lip, frowning, mentally checking over a number of things. Then she went to look for Gilas.

"It's a completely outrageous notion!" her father said a short while later, his tone still somewhat incredulous. He glanced over at Dasinger, who had been listening intently, cleared his throat. "However, let's look at it again. You say you can manufacture 'memories' in the dog's mind which can't be distinguished from things he actually remembers?"

Telzey nodded.

"I can't tell any difference," she said. "And I don't see how a Verifier could."

"Possibly it couldn't," Gilas said. "But we don't really know what such a machine is doing."

"Well, we know what it does in an ethics hearing," Telzey said. "Supposing it did see they were fake memories. What would happen?"

Gilas hesitated, said slowly, "The Verifier would report that it had found nothing to show that the Parlins were connected in any way with the attempt to use Chomir to commit murder. It would report nothing else. It can produce relevant evidence, including visual and auditory effects, to substantiate a claim it has accepted. But it can't explain or show why it is rejecting a claim. To do that would violate the conditions under which it operates."

Dasinger said quietly, "That's it. We can't lose anything. And if it works, we'd have them! Vingarran is the only one who can prove the Parlins never came near his device. But we're keeping him out of sight, and the Parlins can't admit they know he exists without damning themselves! And they can't obtain verification for their own claims of innocence—"

"Because of their mind-blocks!" Gilas concluded. His mouth quirked for an instant; then his face was sober again. "We will, of course, consider every decision. Telzey, go and get Gonwil. We want her in on it, and no one else." He looked at Dasinger. "What will we tell the lawyers?"

Dasinger considered. "That we feel an ethics hearing should be on the record to justify declaring a private war," he said. "They won't like it, of course. They know it isn't necessary."

"No," Gilas agreed, "but it's a good enough excuse. And if they set it up for that purpose, it will cover the steps we'll have to take."

XII

"THE STATEMENTS made by this witness have been neither confirmed nor disproved by verification."

The expressionless face of the chief adjudicator of the Transcluster ethics hearing disappeared from the wall screen of the little observer's cubicle before Telzey as he ended his brief announcement. She frowned, turned her right hand over, palm up, glanced at the slender face of the timepiece in the strap of her wrist-talker.

It had taken less than two minutes for Transcluster's verification machine to establish that it could find nothing in the mind of Rodel Parlin the Twelfth relevent to the subject matter it had been instructed to investigate, and to signal this information to the hearing adjudicators. Junior, visible in the Verifier's contact chamber which showed in the far left section of the screen, had not reacted noticeably to the announcement. It could hardly have been a surprise to him. His parents had preceded him individually to the chamber to have their claims of being innocent of homicidal intentions towards Gonwil Lodis submitted to test, with identical results. Only the stereotyped wording of the report indicated in each case that the machine had encountered mental blocks which made verification impossible. From the Parlins' point of view, that was good enough. The burden of proof rested with their accusers; and they simply had no proof. The demand for an ethics hearing had been a bluff, an attempt perhaps to get a better price for Gonwil's capitulation. If so, it had failed.

The central screen view was shifting back to the hexagonal hall where the Verifier was housed. It appeared almost empty. A technician sat at the single control console near the center, while the machine itself was concealed behind the walls. When he brought it into operation, the far end of the hall came alive with a day-bright blur of shifting radiance, darkening to a sullen red glow as he shut the machine off again. So far, that and the reports of the chief adjudicator had been the only evidence of the Verifier's function; and the play of lights might be merely window dressing, designed to make the proceedings more impressive. It had to be that, Telzey thought, if her speculations about the machine were right. It wasn't really being switched on and off here, but working round the clock, absorbing uncensored information constantly from hundreds of thousands of minds, and passing it on.

But watching the hall darken again as the technician turned away from the console and began to talk into a communicator, Telzey acknowledged to herself that she felt a shade less certain now of the purpose for which the Psychology Service was quietly distributing its psionic machines about the Hub. Gilas was in the observation cubicle next to hers, with two of

Rienne's attorneys; while Gonwil waited with
Dasinger and a few Kyth men in some other section of the great Transcluster Finance complex
for a summons from the adjudicators to take
Chomir to the contact chamber. The hearing had
been under way for a little over an hour.

That was the puzzling point. She had come in
nervously ready for an indication that the Verifier and the human minds behind it knew what
she had been up to before the hearing even began. Her own thoughts were camouflaged; but
Gonwil, Gilas and Dasinger were unconsciously
broadcasting the information that she was a psi
who had manipulated the memories of a hearing
witness in a manner calculated to trick the verification machine into making a false report.

While it was the only way left to get at Malrue,
the Psychology Service certainly must consider
it as flagrant a violation of their rules against the
independent use of psionics as could be imagined. But, so far as Telzey could tell, nothing
happened then ... nothing, at any rate, that
didn't conform in every detail to what was generally assumed to happen at an ethics hearing.
The hearing got off to an unhurried and rather
dull start. One of Rienne's attorneys formally
presented the general charge against the
Parlins—they had planned and attempted to
carry out the murder of Gonwil Lodis for financial gain. He brought out background data on
Lodis Associates to show the motive, displayed
the device used to throw Chomir into a killing
rage, explained the purpose for which similar instruments were employed on Askanam. A description of the occurrence in the Kyth Agency's

hideout followed, including Gonwil's preceding conversation with Junior by the personalized communicator he had sent her, though naturally excluding Telzey's role in checking the dog's attack until a guard had been able to stun him.

Then the specific charge was made. The Parlins had caused the demonstrated device to be used on the dog at a moment when they could assume it would result in Gonwil Lodis's death, leaving no indication that her death had been planned.

From what Telzey had heard, it was the standard sort of introduction. An ethics hearing developed like a game of skill, unfolding from formalized beginnings, and it wasn't until after a few moves and countermoves had been made that significant revelations could be expected. On this occasion, however, the Parlins' attorneys evidently felt they could afford to skip such cautious preliminaries. It was clear now that Vingarran had been captured before he could leave Orado and had talked; but while he presumably would appear as a witness, nothing he knew could endanger the Parlins' position. The attorneys announced that their three principals denied the charges and wished to testify to their innocence under verification if the commercial mind-blocks they employed would permit this.

Having demonstrated then that the mind-blocks, as a matter of fact, did not permit it, the Parlins had retired to wait out the rest of the hearing unchallenged.

Which meant that the next witness up should be Chomir . . .

The use of an animal as a verification witness had been cleared in advance with the adjudicators. It was not without precedent; Chomir would be admitted even if, for some reason, the opposing attorneys objected, and objections weren't expected. The Verifier would be instructed only to establish whether anything could be found in the dog's memory to show the Parlin family had been directly responsible for the murder device planted in his brain.

It was what she had planned. But she had expected to have some intimation by now of what the Verifier's reaction to their doctored witness would be. And there'd been nothing. . . .

Telzey leaned forward suddenly and switched off the central screen and voice transmitters. It might still be several minutes before Chomir was taken to the contact chamber. They'd been told he would be doped first to keep him quiet while the machine carried out its work.

She shifted in the chair, laid her hands, palms down, on the armrests, and closed her eyes. The psi bubble about her mind opened. Her awareness expanded out cautiously into the Transcluster complex.

It wasn't quiet there. Psi whispered, murmured, muttered, in an incessant meaningless trickling from the swarms of humanity which crowded the vast Central. But that seemed to be all. The unaware insect buzz of thousands of minds faded, swelled, faded monotonously; and nothing else happened. She could detect no slightest hint of an active telepath, mechanical or human, nearby.

She didn't know what it meant. She opened

her eyes again, nerves on edge, and as the psi whisperings receded from her awareness, the side screen showed her Chomir already standing in the contact chamber, looking sleepy and bored. She reached out quickly, switched the center screen back on.

Pitch-blackness appeared before her, gleaming with a suggestion of black glass. After a puzzled instant, Telzey realized she must be looking at the projection field within which the Verifier sometimes produced impressions connected with the search it was conducting. The field hadn't come into action when the Parlins were in the chamber; there had been nothing to show. Its appearance in the screen now indicated the machine had begun its work on the dog.

Too late to stop it; she could give Gilas no plausible reason for interrupting the hearing at this point. She watched the screen, waiting, her hands gripping the chair.

There was a sudden strong impression of somebody looking at her. Automatically, Telzey glanced around at the blank wall of the cubicle. No one was there, but the feeling persisted.

Then she knew Transcluster's Verifier had found her.

Her left hand made a panicky flick to her wrist-talker, jabbed down a tiny button. Why had she imagined it would be similar to a human mind, the mind of any living being? This was like being stared at by the sea. And like a vast, cold sea wave it was coming towards her. The bubble snapped tight.

Ordinarily, it might give only a splinter of its attention to the ethics hearings for which it was

upposedly here, and to the relatively unimpor-
ant people involved in them; so perhaps it
vasn't until this moment that it had become
ware some telepathic meddler had been at work
)n the animal mind it was to investigate ...
ind that the meddler was present at the hearing.
n any event, it was after the meddler now.

The cold psi wave reached the bubble, rolled
)ver it, receded, came again. An unprotected
mind must have been flooded in an instant. As it
was, Telzey stayed untouched. It closed over the
bubble again, and now it remained.

It might have lasted only for seconds. There
was a sense of weight building up, of slow, mon-
strous pressures, shifting, purposely applied.
Then the pressures relaxed and withdrew.

The machine mind was still there, watching.
She had the feeling that others watched through
it.

She brought out the thought record she had
prepared for them, and flicked the bubble shielding away from it. And if that let them see she had
never been so scared in her life, the thought record still spoke for itself.

"Take a good look!" she invited.

Almost instantly, she was alone.

Her eyes fastened, somewhat blurrily, on the
projection field in the screen. Colors were boil-
ing up in it. Then there was a jarring sensation of
opening alien eyes and looking out from them.

How it was done Telzey couldn't imagine. But
she, and presumably everyone else watching the
verification field at that moment, was suddenly
aware of being inside Chomir's head. There came

a reddish flash, then a wave of rage building up swiftly to blazing fury. The fury receded again.

A picture came into being, in glimpsed fragments and scraps of almost nightmarish vividness, of the white-walled room in which Chomir had found himself when he awoke with the microscopic Askanam device freshly inserted in his brain. As he had done then, he was pacing swiftly and irritably about the room, the walls and a semi-transparent energy barrier at one end flowing past him in the projection field.

Again came the red flash, followed by the surge of rage. The dog stopped in mid-stride, head swinging towards the barrier. A figure moved vaguely behind the barrier. He hurled himself at it. The barrier flung him back, once, twice. As he came smashing up against it for the third time, the scene suddenly froze.

At this distance, only inches away, the energy field was completely transparent. Three people stood in the section of the room beyond. Rodel Parlin the Twelfth a few feet ahead of his parents, right hand holding an instrument, a small but readily recognizable one. His thumb was on a plunger of the instrument, pressing it down. All three stared at the dog.

The projection field went blank.

For a second, Telzey had the feeling of somebody's screams echoing through her thoughts. It was gone immediately, so she couldn't be sure. But precisely how Malrue Parlin was reacting to what she had just seen in the Verifier's projection field was obviously of no particular importance now.

Telzey put the tip of her left forefinger on the second of the two little buttons she'd had installed recently in her wrist-talker, and pushed it gently down.

A ComWeb chimed persistently. Half awake, Telzey frowned. She had been dreaming, and there seemed to have been something important about the dream because she was trying to hang on to it. But it faded from her awareness like a puff of thin smoke, and she couldn't recall what it had been. She woke up all the way just as the ComWeb went silent.

And where was she? Couch in the semi-dark of a big, comfortable room, rustic type, with the smell of pine trees . . . The far wall was a single window and it was night outside. Moving pinpoints of light and a steadier radiance glittered through a pale, ghostly swirling. . . .

Tor Heights . . .

Of course! Tor Heights, the mountain sports resort . . . in starshine with a snowstorm moving past. With the hearing over, Gilas had suggested she go ahead with Chomir and rent a cabin here, so she and Gonwil could relax from recent stresses for a few days before returning to Pehanron College. He and Gonwil would stay on until the posthearing arrangements with the Transcluster adjudicators and the Parlins' attorneys had been concluded, and then follow. After she'd secured the cabin and fed Chomir, she found herself getting sleepy and curled up for a nap.

That might have been a couple of hours ago.

As she climbed off the couch, the ComWeb began chiming again in the adjoining room.

This time the summons was accompanied by Chomir's attention-requesting rumble. Glancing at her watch, Telzey ran to take the call. She switched on the instrument, and Gonwil's face appeared in the screen, eyes big and sober.

"Hi!" she said. "Your father and I are leaving Draise in about twenty minutes, Telzey. Thought I'd let you know."

"Everything over?" Telzey asked.

"Not quite. They still have a lot of details to settle, but they don't need us around for that. What made it all very simple was that Malrue and Rodel Senior signed up for voluntary Rehabilitation, rather than take Transcluster's penalties." She hesitated, "I almost feel sorry for them now."

"Don't be an idiot," Telzey said thoughtfully. "They've had it coming for years."

"I know. But still . . . well, I couldn't have done it! Not to keep from losing the money."

Telzey admitted she couldn't have done it either. "What about Junior?"

Gonwil smiled briefly. "He wasn't having any! He told the adjudicators that losing his Lodis holdings still would leave him enough to be a playboy the rest of his life, and he couldn't care less about getting placed on Transcluster's black list. The adjudicators said he was practically frothing! Apparently, they were all in a severe state of shock when the hearing ended."

"Glad to hear it," Telzey said. She didn't find herself feeling in the least sorry for the Parlins. "How will you like having Malrue back in Lodis Associates after they let her out of rehabilitation?"

"I don't know just how I would feel about it," Gonwil said, "but I won't be there when she comes back. That ruling's been canceled, and I'm selling to the Bank of Rienne. I decided I'm not really cut out to be a Tayun financier. Besides, I've . . . oh, started to develop other interests."

"Like in the Federation Navy?" Telzey asked.

Gonwil colored slightly. "Perhaps."

After she had switched off, Telzey found and pushed the button which started the big fire place in the main room going, then another button which let the sound of the soft, roaring rush of the storm pass through the cabin. She got a glass of milk and sat down reflectively with it before the fire.

Of course, the Parlins had realized they'd lost the hearing as soon as they saw themselves in the projection field. They must have nearly gone out of their minds for a while. But they couldn't prove they'd never been in such a room with Chomir, and to dispute a Verifier's report was useless. What had happened seemed impossible! But they were trapped, and they knew it.

Nevertheless, Telzey thought, it was very unlikely the senior Parlins would have preferred rehabilitation to losing their Lodis stock—if it had been left up to them. That was what had jolted Gonwil: she knew such a decision didn't really go with the kind of people they were. But it couldn't be explained to her, or to anybody else, that the decision hadn't been their own.

Telzey sipped meditatively at her milk. Clear and obvious in the thought record she'd displayed to the Verifier, and to whatever Psychology Service agents were studying her through their machine, was the information that unless a certain thing was done and certain other things were not done, vast numbers of copies of a report she'd deposited in a non-direct mailing vault would be dumped into the non-direct system within minutes, tagged with randomly selected delivery dates extending up to fifteen years in the future.

On any day, during that fifteen-year period, there might show up at some of the Hub's more prominent news services a concise statement, with data appended, of every significant fact she had deduced or suspected concerning psis and psionics in the Hub, and particularly of the role the Psychology Service and its psionic machines appeared to be playing. The first such missive to reach its destination should make quite a splash throughout the Hub. . . .

So she'd blackmailed a department of the Overgovernment, and while they mightn't relish it much, frankly, it felt good. Among the things they weren't to do was to try to take control of her, mentally or physically. And the thing to be done, of course, was to see to it that the Parlins were found guilty at the ethics hearing of the crime they'd planned, even though the methods of convicting them might be open to question.

Considering the Verifier's ability to scan minds at large, they must have been aware by then that the Parlins were guilty, though they wouldn't have lifted a finger to help out Gonwil if they hadn't been forced to it. Being forced to it, they turned in a fast, artistic job, using Telzey's fabrication but adding a number of lifelike touches she couldn't have provided, and presenting it in a convincing dramatic manner.

Then they'd had to take immediate additional action to keep the stunned Parlins from wailing loudly enough to raise doubts about the infallibility of the ethics hearing procedures. As she knew from experience, the psionic machines were very good at installing on-the-spot compulsions.

So Malrue and her husband had applied for rehabilitation. The machines in the rehabilitation center would take it from there. The Psychology Service might have exempted Junior as being too much of a lightweight to worry about, but they certainly had seen to it that he wouldn't do any talking.

So far, so good, Telzey thought. She put down the glass of milk and slipped off her shoes. Chomir had strolled in from the next room and settled himself in front of her, and she placed her feet on his back now, kneading the thick, hard slabs of muscle with toes and heels. He grunted comfortably.

Gonwil's difficulties were over. And now where did she stand with the Psychology Service?

She considered it a while. Essentially, they seemed to be practical people, so they shouldn't be inclined to hold grudges. But she would look like a problem to them.

She'd reduced the problem as much as possible. Letting somebody look into sections of your mind was a good deal more satisfactory than making promises when you were out to create an atmosphere of confidence. If they had seen what you really intended, they didn't worry about cheating.

The Psychology Service knew now she wouldn't give away any of their secrets unless they forced her to it—which again was a practical decision on her part. She couldn't talk about them to Gonwil or her parents or Dasinger because their minds would be an open book any time they came near a psionic machine, and if she had told them too much, they might be in trouble then.

And in her own interest, she had no intention of telling people in general what she knew about psis—not, at least, until she understood a great deal more of what she'd be talking about.

Again, so far, so good.

Then there was the matter of having threatened to use the nondirect mailing system to expose them. She hadn't let them see whether she intended to give up that arrangement or not. As a matter of fact, the package of prepared reports had been destroyed shortly before she set off for Tor Heights, because of the risk of something going wrong accidentally and, not inconceivably, changing the course of Federation history as a result. They probably had expected her to do it, but they couldn't be sure. And even if they were, they didn't know what else she might have cooked up.

So the probability was they would decide it was wisest to leave her alone as long as she didn't disturb their plans. For her part, she would be very happy to leave them alone providing they didn't start trying to run her life again.

No doubt, they could have taught her what she wanted to know about psionics; but their price looked like more than she was willing to pay. And she didn't seem to be doing too badly at teaching herself.

The Federation of the Hub was a vast area, after all. Aside from occasional contacts with their mechanized spy network, there was no real reason, Telzey concluded, why she and the Psychology Service should ever run into each other again.

Satisfied, she reached around for a couch cushion, placed it behind her neck, wriggled into a different position, laid her head back and closed her eyes. Might as well go on napping until Gilas and Gonwil arrived. On checking in here, she'd been told that float-ski conditions were perfect, so tomorrow should be a strenuous day. . . .

Abruptly, she found herself sitting bolt upright again, eyes wide open, while Chomir grumbled at her feet about all this shifting around.

She had drifted straight back into the dream out of which the ComWeb had roused her twenty minutes before. It had been another dream about the Psionic Cop. He'd appeared almost completely faded out, hardly more than a transparent outline of what he'd been; and Telzey had informed him, perhaps a trifle smugly, that he might just as well vanish for good now. Since she'd let the Psychology Service know she could block out snoopers, there was no further point in his hanging around her.

And the ghostly Cop had nodded very seriously, and said, "Yes, we were greatly pleased to discover you had been able to develop such an effective defensive measure, Miss Amberdon! It was one of the things we had to find out about you. You see, it will be necessary . . ."

Telzey bit her lip uneasily, staring at the quietly dancing fire, listening to the soft moan of the snow winds over Tor Heights. An eerie little chill began to slide up and down her spine.

It had been just a dream—probably! It didn't have to mean anything.

But supposing it hadn't been just a dream . . .?

Necessary—*for what?*

About the Author. . . .

James Henry Schmitz was born in Hamburg, Germany in 1911 of American parents, and moved to the U.S. in 1938. He worked in harvester and trailer building, first in Germany and then in the U.S., and served with the U.S.A.F. in the Pacific during World War II. In 1959 he turned to a full-time writing career. His first published science fiction story, "Greenface", appeared in *Unknown* in 1943. In the 1960s, when the majority of his novels were written and published, Mr. Schmitz firmly established himself as one of the leading writers in the field. He is perhaps best known for his delightful novel *The Witches of Karres,* and for his consistent use of strong female protagonists at a time when science fiction was a male-oriented genre.

THE WORLDS OF H. BEAM PIPER

_____	20557-7 EMPIRE	$2.50
_____	23190-X FEDERATION	$2.95
_____	23920-X FIRST CYCLE	$2.50
	(edited and expanded by Michael Kurland)	
_____	24892-6 FOUR-DAY PLANET AND LONE STAR PLANET	$2.95
_____	26176-0 FUZZIES AND OTHER PEOPLE	$2.95
_____	26182-5 FUZZY BONES William Tuning	$2.95
_____	26195-7 FUZZY SAPIENS	$2.75
_____	29727-7 GOLDEN DREAM: A FUZZY ODYSSEY Ardath Mayhar	$2.95
_____	48497-2 LITTLE FUZZY	$2.75
_____	49055-7 LORD KALVAN OF OTHERWHEN	$2.75
_____	65170-4 PARATIME	$2.95
_____	84292-5 ULLER UPRISING	$2.75
_____	91053-X THE WORLDS OF H. BEAM PIPER	$2.75
_____	77784-8 SPACE VIKING	$2.75

Prices may be slightly higher in Canada.